# *H*eart
## of a
# Woman

*Gael Morrison*

*Heart of a Woman* is a work of fiction. Names, characters and incidents are products of the author's imagination or are used fictitiously. Any resemblance to actual events or locales or persons, living or dead, is entirely coincidental.

Published 2003 by
The Fiction Works
Lake Tahoe, Nevada
www.fictionworks.com

Copyright © 2002
by Gael Morrison

ISBN 1-58124-703-6
Printed in the
United States of America

*Dedicated with love to*

*My mother and father,*
*Ruby and John Friesen,*
*    sailors of the South seas*

*and to*

*Jann Crowley*
*    whose heart is an inspiration*

# Heart
## of a
# Woman

# Chapter One

Tearing his gaze from Jann Fletcher's disconcertingly blue eyes, Peter Strickland ushered her into his lawyer's office.

"My lawyer, Mr. Moore," he murmured.

The Fletcher woman glanced at Moore, nodded, then turned back to Peter, frowning. Her long cotton skirt and wispy blouse seemed more suited to the beach than to an upscale Honolulu lawyer's office.

"Have a seat," Peter said, directing her to one of Moore's black leather chairs. "I appreciate you meeting me on such short notice."

Somehow he was able to stop himself searching the space beyond her, knowing already there was no baby carriage parked against the wall in the corridor outside. The need to see his sister's baby, to touch him, to truly believe he existed had driven Peter mad in the week since Jann Fletcher's letter had arrived. Only seven days, but they'd been filled with paperwork, lawyers and travel arrangements.

"I hoped you would bring Alexander with you," he said.

"It's Alex's nap time," she replied, her voice warm and slow with the lilting drawl of an islander.

It should have been sharper, Peter thought, and crisper, should have matched her red hair.

"Besides . . ." The frown lines on her forehead deepened. "I don't know why you asked me here."

"I wanted to thank you," Peter said stiffly, not liking his obligation to this woman. "I wanted to tell you in person how grateful I am for all you've done for my nephew." He banished Claire from his mind, not wanting to think of his sister now, wanting only to concentrate on her baby.

"It was my pleasure."

"It must have been difficult."

"No," she denied, the lie obvious in the pain angling through her eyes, smudging their blue with blackness.

"A young woman like you, single." As his sister had been single. Peter cleared his throat. "The last six months can't have been easy." If he kept his mind focused on Jann Fletcher's hardships, he might stop thinking of Claire's, of how alone his sister must have felt, how frightened.

"Alex has been no problem," the woman said.

"Just the same, I'm grateful. Grateful, too, that you wrote."

"It seemed the right thing to do." She gave him a faint smile.

It lit the room, her smile, Peter thought dazedly.

"I knew the lawyers would inform you," she went on, her smile now fading, "but that's a terrible way to find out."

"Yes," he said, his shoulders stiffening. He still prayed that he'd wake and find he had dreamed the whole thing; that it was a nightmare, not a reality.

"You'll want to visit Alex now you're here," Jann said, sitting straighter in her chair.

"Visit? I'm not here to visit. I've come to collect Alexander."

"Collect him?"

"I'm taking him back to Boston with me."

"Taking him? What do you mean?"

"Alexander is my nephew. Naturally, he'll live with me."

"No!" Her voice was low, but she gripped the arms of her chair, her fingers digging into the black leather.

"I want to give Alexander a home." Like the one he and Claire had enjoyed as children, until their mother changed and abandoned Claire without a backward glance.

Jann shook her head, but was unable to pull her gaze from Peter Strickland's eyes. Claire hadn't mentioned they were the color of emeralds, although she'd said plenty on the subject of her brother.

"I won't be taking him today, of course."

"You won't be taking him at all."

"You'll need time to get his things packed, to say your good-byes."

Jann fought back the panic rising in her chest. Surely this man couldn't mean what he was saying. Not looking as he did. Not staring at her with Claire's eyes.

Alex's eyes, too.

"I can understand you wanting to spend time with Alex—"

"I do," Peter said. "I haven't even seen him yet."

"He's already six months old." She could hear the criticism lacing her voice, the implication that if he'd truly cared, he'd have known where his sister was, would have been there to help her.

"I know." His lips tightened. "But I didn't know Claire was dead. I didn't know where she had disappeared to until I got your letter."

And was furious about that, Jann realized. She should have listened to Claire, should never have contacted her friend's brother. But she hadn't realized until now that he would want her baby.

"I'm sure you've become attached to Alexander," Strickland continued in a gentler voice, "but I know you'll be happy to be free of the responsibility, relieved to get back to your own life."

The air fled Jann's lungs, leaving her dizzy. Claire's brother's lips still moved, but his voice had disappeared beneath the buzzing in her ears.

"I hope you'll accept a token of my gratitude."

His voice had become clear again, too clear, as though all other sounds had died, leaving only his words and the horror they promised. He pulled an envelope from his jacket pocket and held it out towards her.

"No," Jann said again, in a lower voice than before, but the word reverberated in her head like a scream.

"You've been very kind, Ms Fletcher, but I insist."

"I mean 'no' you may not have custody of Alex."

"I'm his uncle," he said again, as though this was something he wasn't sure she understood. "If not me, who?"

"Me. Claire gave Alex to me."

He frowned. "She had no business asking such a thing of you. She was too young herself to know what a responsibility he would be."

"She knew," Jann said firmly, moisture pricking her eyes.

"Mr. Moore has started the paperwork." Strickland gestured toward his lawyer sitting dwarfed behind his desk, his papers spread before him like soldiers on parade. "When you've thought this through, you'll see it's for the best."

"There's nothing to think through."

"You can't seriously want the responsibility of caring for a child?"

"That's exactly what I do want." The disbelief in his eyes unnerved Jann. She rose from her chair, wishing she were taller, wishing she could stand eyeball to eyeball with this man.

"It doesn't have to be the end of your relationship with Alexander." Strickland's expression grew gentler, his eyes sympathetic. "Honolulu's a long way from Boston, but we can work something out. Fly you over once a year—"

"I don't want to fly to Boston once a year. Or even twice a year. I want Alex with me all the time. You can fly here if you want to visit him."

Strickland seemed to grow even taller than he had been before. "I'm afraid that's not possible."

His gravelly voice skittered shivers across Jann's shoulders. He paced the length and breadth of the office while he spoke, as though unable to keep still. Then he turned back to his lawyer, his black hair lifting with the movement.

"I want you to file that custody application today, Mr. Moore. I don't want to stay here . . ." Strickland's gaze flickered out the office window toward the downtown Honolulu street. ". . . any longer than necessary."

Jann swept her strawberry curls away from her face and jerked back her shoulders, wishing she had tied her hair in a bun, had tried to look older, more responsible.

She had dressed inappropriately, too. Her loose-fitting Indian blouse and gauzy skirt were comfortable, but—she glanced at the tie knotted impeccably around Strickland's neck—she should have worn a tailored suit.

If she had owned one, she would have. If she had known beforehand what this meeting was about.

"You can file all the legal suits you want," she declared, "but nobody . . ." Her throat rasped raw as she attempted to clear it. ". . . nobody is going to take my baby away from me."

"Your baby?" Strickland's accent suddenly seemed more British than Bostonian.

"Yes, mine." Little Alex was hers. Claire had said so.

No. Claire had insisted.

Strickland's gaze swept over Jann, seemed to linger at her waist before flashing past her breasts to meet her eyes. "You didn't give birth to Alexander. I fail to see how you can claim him."

Claire had given her that claim. Claire, sitting on their special bench in the park, calmly asking Jann to be her delivery coach.

Jann had argued with Claire, reasoned with her, tried everything rather than become involved. But in the end she had agreed. There hadn't been anyone else.

"I was there when Alex was born," she explained in a low voice. Born. Such a simple word for a miracle.

"As were the doctors and nurses, but they aren't here laying claim to my sister's child."

"Claire didn't give them custody."   Jann's hand stole upward to the heart-shaped crystal hanging from her neck. Her mother had given it to her, the last thing she'd given her. Its smooth surface usually soothed Jann. But not today. Her pulse was racing as fast as a fox's before a hound.

"Claire was obviously not in her right mind—"

"You don't know anything about the state of your sister's mind." Heat swept Jann's cheeks.

Peter Strickland's eyes darkened. "It wouldn't be the first time she made a poor decision."

"How would you know? You were off in Asia or Africa somewhere."

"She left home—"

"You could hardly call it a home."

". . . moved into a slummy apartment in New York . . ." A muscle rippled along his jaw line.

"Which you never saw."

". . . ran around with people who'd have been better off in jail . . ."

"She had no one else."

". . . drank, did drugs . . ."

It sounded ugly. Jann shuddered. Was ugly. But didn't he care why Claire had done it?

". . . and got pregnant with a man not fit to breathe her air."

Jann took a step closer, her skirt swirling around her legs. Her arms hung straight at her sides and her fingernails bit her palms. She felt like a thin wisp of nothing next to Peter Strickland's bulk and muscle.

"It doesn't matter what sort of man Alex's father was," Jann began, moving forward another step. "What matters is who his mother was."

The man before her flinched.

"And that's Claire—your sister—in case you've forgotten." Tears filled Jann's eyes, reducing Strickland's image to a series of squiggly lines. "My friend," she added softly, then swept away the tears. She would not cry in front of this man. He would think she was afraid. He wouldn't know her tears were for Claire.

She was very close to him now. He reached out his hand as though intending to grasp her shoulder, but at the last instant stopped, his fingers warm as they brushed her arm.

"I've not forgotten Claire is Alexander's mother," he began, his eyes burning with a pain Jann understood too well. "There's no likelihood of my ever forgetting that."

"Or forgiving it either," Jann accused.

He sucked in a deep breath, seemed to be collecting his thoughts as to how to deal best with an emotional female. "Don't worry about Alexander," he finally went on, ignoring her accusation. "I'll take good care of him. I promise."

"I promised Claire I would never give him up." She stood as tall as she was able. "I never break my promises."

"You're going to have to break this one." He waved his hand in the direction of Mr. Moore. "You won't want to fight this out in court."

Jann glanced at the lawyer sitting behind the oak desk. His face was expressionless, looking as dry and unfeeling as the laws he upheld.

She didn't want to go to court, couldn't face such an ordeal again. Her chest tightened. Courts made decisions, and they weren't always the right ones. In the past, they had never been the right ones for her.

"You don't want to throw away your money," Strickland went on, dragging Jann's attention back to what he was saying.

"Money?"

"If you intend to fight, Ms Fletcher, it's going to cost you in legal fees. Are you prepared for that?" He looked at her as though he knew to a penny all she had or ever would have.

Her spirits sank. He was right in his knowledge that she had no money, but the thought of Alex, with his soft skin and laughing eyes, strengthened her resolve.

"If it's a fight you want," she said tightly, "then it's a fight you'll get." She'd pay for it somehow. Take that assignment on Molokai if she had to.

Strickland's eyes narrowed. "Why do you care so much?" His question seemed sincere, but he held himself stiffly, as though already distrusting whatever answer she would give.

"I promised his mother," she repeated, pushing away the image of Claire on her deathbed, not wanting ever again to think of her friend like that.

"I'm sure you've done your best," he said, brushing away her promise as though it meant nothing, "but Alexander is my nephew, my blood. He belongs with me."

"He belongs with someone who loves him. And that's me," she said firmly.

"Perhaps it's time we concluded this meeting," Mr. Moore broke in saying.

Jann was unable to move, unable to breathe, unable even to wrench her gaze away.

"Alexander is mine," Claire's brother insisted.

"He's not a possession," she cried, rage erupting as suddenly as a Tsunami at sea, blowing the lid off emotions she'd suppressed for years.

Until Claire died.

Until now.

"He's a little baby," she protested. "He needs love. My love." Even if loving Alex went against everything she had learned in the twelve years since her parents had died, that she could only be safe if she kept herself to herself.

Mr. Moore noisily shifted some papers on his desk, but Peter Strickland's gaze didn't stray from hers. It didn't seem possible his eyes could become darker, but they did, the soft fullness of his lashes incongruous frames for their sharpness. Like feathers around steel.

Jann struggled to get a sense of his aura, of what he was feeling and what he would say. But her own senses seemed to have shut down, for around Peter Strickland she could discern nothing but a black mist.

"Love isn't the issue," he said, leaning forward as he spoke, drawing so near his breath warmed her cheek. "Not with you."

"What do you mean?"

"How much do you want?" His voice had hardened, become businesslike.

But he smelled like the earth after a rain, Jann thought dazedly. Crisp, clean, and good.

"Well?"

She couldn't think, couldn't concentrate on what he was saying. Not when he was this close.

"How much would it take for you to disappear?"

"Money?" she asked, suddenly understanding.

"Of course, money. Five thousand? Ten thousand?"

"Dollars?"

"You drive a hard bargain, but fifteen thousand is as high as I go."

"You think I would sell Alex?" She couldn't believe his suggestion, was sure her ears deceived.

"I'm sure you have your price." His expression held no surprise, but rather disappointment, as though he was sure what her answer would be. "It's what you've been waiting for, isn't it?"

"What do you mean?"

"Why else would you be so interested in raising my sister's

son?" His jaw hardened. "You knew what she was worth. Now she's dead her baby inherits the lot."

Jann opened her mouth but no words emerged. It was as if he had wrapped a steel band around her chest and was tightening its pressure until it squeezed her in two.

"Well?" he prodded.

She tried again. "I can't believe you think I'm doing this for money."

"I didn't at first." His lips tightened. "I do now."

"If you believe that . . ." She lifted her chin. ". . . then you know nothing about me or your sister."

"I know your type."

"What do you mean type?"

"My sister surrounded herself with people like you. People who used her to get what they wanted. You had me fooled, too."

His words were like bullets hitting her square between the eyes.

"My sister didn't know any better, had never been taught." He stopped suddenly and caught his breath, as though he had more to say, but couldn't bear to utter the words.

"You're attractive," he finally went on. "I'm surprised you haven't linked up with some rich old man. Easier, surely, than caring for a baby."

"You can think what you like."

"Your hair's an unusual color. If you need money, I understand beauty salons pay well to turn hair like yours into wigs."

"If you've completely finished," Jann said, her fingers forming fists. Claire's brother might dress like a gentleman and have the eyes of an angel, but he didn't play by the rules.

"Although your clothes will never do," he continued, ignoring her interruption. "That flower child look went out in the sixties." One brow lifted. "But perhaps that's part of the con. Work the sympathy element and force the sucker from back east into paying more."

Jann squeezed her eyes shut. She'd faced a lot in her life, but this man was hard.

"So, Ms Fletcher, what's your price?"

Opening her eyes, she met his gaze squarely. "You don't have that kind of money," she said, exhilaration surging through her at the surprise sweeping across his face. "The only thing I'll settle for is one . . . small . . . baby."

"I don't believe that."

"Believe it. If it takes everything I have, I'm keeping Alex."

"I've underestimated you, Ms Fletcher. Not a mistake I often make."

"What do you mean?"

"You're after it all." His lips pulled back in disgust. "Alexander's your ticket to the good life. No court in the land would object to you spending money to keep him in the style to which he's entitled."

"I've spent very little!" Before Alex was born, Claire had already purchased a crib and high chair, a changing table and a car seat, too.

"Though there have been some expenses. Formula . . ." This time it was impossible to fight back the image of Claire lying in her hospital bed breast-feeding her newborn son. A few short days were all they'd had together. Idyllic days before Claire got sick.

". . . and diapers." Every time Jann turned around, Alex was wet. "Clothes," she continued firmly. "I've sewn him some smocks, but he's getting bigger. He's going to need clothes to crawl around in soon." She reached for the high back of her leather chair and held on to it for support. "You're being unfair. The little I've spent money on, Alex has needed. That's what his trust fund is for after all."

Claire's brother shrugged his shoulders. "It's a small step from necessities to luxuries. Of course you'd keep it down until your custody claim was assured, then . . ."

"Here!" Jann cried, snatching up the bag she'd left next to her chair, a multi-colored woven one a friend had brought her from Greece. With trembling fingers, she rummaged in its depths. Finally, she felt the metal clip amongst a multitude of wrinkled papers, and with a sharp tug, extricated a stack of invoices from the bottom of her bag.

She flung the papers onto Moore's desk. "You'll find every penny I've spent accounted for in these receipts."

"Really, Miss Fletcher," Strickland's lawyer began, "you're not required at this time to show us an itemized account."

"No?" Jann turned and looked at Claire's brother. "Then it seems I've misunderstood Mr. Strickland. I thought he'd be relieved to know no one is interested in cheating Alex." Her voice caught. "Least of all, me."

"So you say," Peter replied. "But until I gain custody, my eyes will be on you."

Scrutinizing her. Watching. A trembling began in the pit of Jann's stomach and traveled at lightning speed through the rest of her body. No privacy. No freedom. No escape. She'd already been through it a long time ago, and had never forgotten how it felt. She couldn't do it again.

When Claire had refused to inform her brother of her illness and the very real possibility she might not survive, Jann had been aghast. She'd been convinced that no matter how imperfect the relationship between them was, Claire's brother should be there, if only to care for Alex when the time came.

But Claire had been adamant. Her brother would never understand, she had said.

Jann stared up at Peter Strickland.

It seemed Claire was right.

# Chapter Two

Jann glanced down at Alex. One chubby arm flailed upward, but he didn't open his eyes. Even while sleeping, his hair, as black and thick as his uncle's, stood straight up from his head. Too much hair for a baby, she thought, and so wild, as though an eggbeater had whipped it into a twirling frenzy.

It was tough enough learning to care for a small baby properly, terrified she'd make a mistake, that something vital would go amiss, but if Peter Strickland made good his threat to watch her, something was bound to go wrong.

She trundled Alex's buggy down the short flight of steps leading to her friend Mitch's basement law office, then awkwardly swung open the door.

Betty, Mitch's secretary, glanced up from her computer keyboard and peered over the top of her bifocals. "Let's see that little angel," she cooed, flashing Jann a welcoming smile as she pushed back her chair and stood.

Jann smothered the smile of pride she'd been finding on her face lately and stood aside as Betty moved to Alex's buggy and lifted the baby out. His face puckered like that of a worried old man.

"Come on, doll," Betty crooned. "I'll show you around the office while your mommy talks business." She gestured toward her boss's office. "Go on in Jann. Mitch is expecting you."

Jann edged between the buggy and a hair-groping monkey fern and headed down the hall. Mitch would tell her she and Alex were safe. He was sure to. In all the years she'd known him, he had never let her down.

She pushed open his door. Sunlight poured in through a picture window, warming the pale green walls and the multitude of plants threatening to engulf the small amount of space not taken up by books. Mitch, tall, bearded, and infinitely comforting, rose to greet her.

"Well," Jann said, hating the worry lacing her voice, "what do you think?"

"I phoned Richard Moore," Mitch replied, gesturing to the chair in front of his desk. His usually genial face was sober. "There are no guarantees, Jann, that Claire's custody wishes will be upheld."

Jann's heart thudded against her rib cage. "But why, Mitch? Claire left Alex to me."

"I know, Jann," he said softly. "I have the custody papers right here. But Peter Strickland has the right to file for custody."

"But the documents make Claire's wishes perfectly clear."

"They do . . ." Mitch's voice, as usual, was as soothing as a warm wind through a palm tree.

Only this time, Jann didn't feel soothed.

". . . but custody cases are decided on what's in the best interest of the child."

"Alex will be best off with me."

"That'll be for the courts to decide." Mitch's brown eyes filled with sympathy and his pen beat an erratic tune on his desk.

"So Peter Strickland has a chance?" Fear constricted Jann's throat.

"Yes."

The single word exploded like a bomb in her head.

"He's filed for custody," Mitch continued, "although the hearing won't be for at least four months." He grimaced. "It usually takes much longer than that. Moore's obviously pulled in some favors."

Moore was probably the best lawyer money could buy. Jann glanced across the desk at her friend. Money wasn't everything. She'd rather pin her faith on a lawyer with a heart.

It was all she had.

"So we have four months," she said, worriedly chewing her lower lip. "That's a long time. Peter Strickland surely won't want to stay in Honolulu forever. Perhaps he'll return to Boston until the custody hearing." The tension in her shoulders eased at the thought of Peter leaving.

"I don't think so," Mitch said regretfully.

"What do you mean?"

"He's applied for access."

"Access!" She swept her tongue across suddenly dry lips. "He won't get it will he? What kind of a system do we have, for God's sake, when any Tom, Dick or Harry can apply for access?"

"He is the baby's uncle," Mitch reminded her gently. "He does have rights."

"He gave up on those rights when he gave up on Claire." She placed her hands flat on the desk. "Can we oppose this access application?"

"We could," Mitch said, "but you have to decide if it'll do you any good in the long run."

"What do you mean?"

"How will the courts view your blocking the uncle's opportunity to get to know his nephew? They may not look favorably on that. They'll wonder why you're doing it."

"So what do you suggest?"

"Well, it's up to you, of course, but you might wish to agree to the access."

"I don't want that man anywhere near Alex. What if he tries to take him out of Hawaii?"

"Kidnap him, you mean?" Mitch's eyebrows rose.

"Yes," Jann said firmly. "You've not met Peter Strickland. He's the sort of man who takes what he wants."

"We could suggest supervised access."

"What does that mean?"

"You'd be with him whenever he's with Alex."

"Impossible!" The very idea filled her with horror.

"Before you decide," Mitch said, "there's one more thing you should consider."

"What's that?"

"If he does go to court, they may well award him unsupervised access. If you offer him something enticing, it may be enough to keep the question out of court."

"Like what?" She braced herself.

"Unlimited supervised access. It may pay you to be generous, especially as the man presumably has a business to run. He won't want to be restricted to one afternoon every two weeks. With unlimited access, he may spend a lot of time with Alex for the next week or two, then return to Boston until the custody hearing."

Jann put her face in her hands, willing her brain to stop its whirling. Finally, reluctantly, she lifted her head and nodded.

Mitch was right.


Peter's steps began to drag the instant he entered the park. He wanted it to be over, wanted to grab hold of Claire's son and take him home to safety. Away from this island.

Away from that woman.

Where the hell was she?

There. Just where she had said she would be, looking as elusive as a tree sprite standing beneath those pink blossoms, her cotton dress shimmering in shades of mauve and green. His mother used to wear a dress that color, only hers was made of silk. He'd always loved it, had felt enveloped by her colors into a land of magic and laughter. Got sucked in, in the process.

"Good morning, Ms Fletcher," he said, stepping off the path onto the grass. He'd forgotten how blue her eyes were— the same color as the sky. They were watching him. "So you've decided to be reasonable?"

Color swept her cheeks. "It's only fair to Alex that he see you while you're here."

"He'll be coming with me when I go."

"I wouldn't count on that, Mr. Strickland."

Her eyes held the same defiant look Claire's had always held. A look that had secretly filled him with pride, though his parents had tried to break his sister of it. He hadn't. He'd figured the defiance and the courage that went with it would keep Claire safe, would provide a barrier against trusting too much, against giving her heart too easily. Peter swallowed hard. He'd been wrong, and because of it his sister was lying in a grave on an island in the Pacific.

"If we're going to spend time together, you'd better call me Peter," he said, in a voice so tight he scarcely recognized it as his own.

She said nothing.

"Where is Alexander?" He needed to see the child, hold him, find a piece of Claire still left on earth.

"Alex is at home . . ."

The woman was looking like Claire again, all bristly and cross.

". . . where he belongs."

"I expected you to bring him with you this time."

"You don't always get what you expect."

"I'd like to see him."

"Not yet. We have to talk first."

"We did enough of that the other day."

"We have to lay some ground rules."

She couldn't be as sure of herself as she sounded. She stood behind the bench as though she needed its protection.

"Come out of hiding then," he said, offering her his hand.

Ignoring it, she walked around to where he stood. She had seemed taller, somehow, standing on her own. Now the top of her head barely reached his chin.

He motioned her onto the park bench, then sat down himself, as far from her as possible. He couldn't get too near. Something about her attracted him, and he had no intention of falling under the spell of a woman like her. "Claire would have loved this park," he said, looking around at the lush, well-tended greenery.

"She did," Jann answered. "She said the trees were different, but they still reminded her of home."

"She liked to climb trees," Peter said, remembering. "She climbed to the top of a maple tree once." And he'd stood beneath ready to catch her if she fell.

Only he hadn't caught her when she really needed him. After his parents died he'd let her go, and her free fall to disaster had been final and swift.

Peter straightened his shoulders. He would not allow the same thing to happen to Claire's son.

"So?" he asked tersely, shifting the conversation back to the business at hand.

"You've agreed then, to supervised access?"

"Unlimited supervised access, yes." Not nearly enough, but it would do for the moment.

Her blue eyes clouded. Reaching down, she snapped off a blade of grass and twirled it between thumb and forefinger. Her hair now hid her face like a veil of fire. She seemed too young to care for a baby, but when she faced him again, he saw that her eyes were old. "You do know you can't see Alex without my being present?" she said.

"Why?" he asked, more sharply than he would have if he hadn't suddenly wanted to touch her, to smooth the worry lines away from her brow. "Are you afraid I'm going to make off with him?"

"Yes."

She didn't trust him, but he didn't blame her for that. He

didn't trust her either.

"You keep an eye on me," he suggested, "and I'll keep an eye on you." He leaned back against the bench, tried to steel himself against her appealing magnetism. "The court will need reasons to deny you permanent custody. I intend to find them."

"There are no reasons," she protested, turning pale.

He tried not to care but couldn't stop a rush of sympathy. He'd had Moore check up on her. She had no family, few close friends. Without Alexander, she'd have no one.

He knew how that felt. Since being informed of Claire's death he, too, had felt alone. He couldn't allow Claire's baby to feel the same. He had to gain custody, had to keep Alexander safe.

"If I were you," Jann Fletcher went on, "I'd concentrate on how you're going to prove you'll make the better parent, because as far as I'm concerned, you have a lot of proving to do."

"I was like a parent to Claire."

"She didn't say that," Jann replied.

"She knew it nonetheless." Pain threatened to choke him, and along with it came anger.

He'd been ten when Claire was born, young enough to be thrilled by the thought of a baby sister, old enough to be entranced by her crinkly smile and helpless need. He'd played with her, read her bedtime stories, had done all the things his parents were never around to do. Claire had meant more to him than to anyone else, as he had to her.

Until he failed her. Peter pressed his lips together. That wasn't going to happen twice.

"As soon as the court realizes," he continued, "that my sister was not in a proper state of mind when she died, they'll give Alexander to me."

"What makes you think Claire wasn't thinking straight?"

Jann demanded.

"Surely that's obvious. She was a well-brought-up young woman from a respected family." His hands clenched into fists but with deliberate effort, he managed to force them straight. His sister had been too young, thank God, to understand the scenes that had left him shaken. The stormy arguments between their parents, their sudden silences, their frequent absences, sometimes one, sometimes the other.

It was usually his mother who disappeared, dispensing absent-minded hugs then airily trailing off with the latest in a line of incense-burning, sitar-strumming friends, taking her warmth and laughter with her as she went.

"When my parents were alive . . ." Peter stared off into the distance, determined that Claire's friend see no pain in his eyes.

"Things change," Jann said softly.

Yes, they did. Too much. But he wasn't about to discuss family matters with her.

"Your parents died," she prompted.

"Yes," he said tightly. Too soon to realize they owed their children more than money. "Claire always wanted to live in Willow House," he went on. "I know she'd want her child to be brought up there too."

"Willow House?"

"Our country home outside of Boston. It's been in my family for generations. I own it now. It's where we will live. Alexander and myself." His parents had been happy there once, as he and Claire had, too, before their mother became enraptured by her pleasure-seeking life and their father refused to follow her flower-strewn path.

"Alexander is happy here with me."

"He'll love Willow House as much as Claire did."

"Who took care of Claire when your parents died?" Jann asked.

"She moved in with my aunt and uncle. She was surrounded by her family."

"She said she was alone."

"It was Claire who left." But she'd left because he hadn't been there to stop her. A pain clenched his gut. "If she hadn't, she'd have been safe."

"No one is ever safe," Jann whispered.

"Safer than running around New York with vagrants and drunks. Becoming like them. Losing sight of who she was."

"Is that what you consider important?" Jann looked at him pityingly. "Who she was, her background, her place in society?"

"That's not what I meant." Only one thing was important—that Claire wasn't there anymore—would never be there again. "Claire's background should have kept her safe, would have if she had let it. She was too trusting, was always being taken in by con-artists. She believed all sorts of sob stories." God alone knew what the woman beside him had convinced his sister to believe. Those blue eyes worked their magic even on him!

"If she had remembered who she was," he went on fiercely, "and what she had, she would never have gotten involved with the wrong kind of people, the wrong kind of man . . ." His skin felt tight, as though his insides had grown too large for his body. ". . . or allowed herself to get pregnant."

"She wasn't ashamed of that."

"What do you mean?" He took hold of Jann's arm, intending not to let go until he understood, but the minute he touched her, he wished that he hadn't. For touching her ignited a warmth he shouldn't feel, not for this woman who had his sister's child.

Her bare skin burned where Peter's hand held hers. His fingers were warm and dry, and . . . powerful, not cold like his eyes were at this minute.

"Claire was ecstatic about being pregnant," Jann said, shrugging herself free, ignoring the inexplicable loss when they no longer touched. "She glowed with happiness."

Peter glowered.

"When I first met her—"

"Where was that?"

"Not at some drug party, whatever you might think!" She gazed over the lawns rolling toward the ocean and attempted a smile. "Right here," she finally said, trying vainly to capture the peace of the place.

"What do you mean, here?"

She stroked the smooth wood beneath her. "When I bike through the park in the morning, I usually stop at this bench to eat breakfast."

"Breakfast?"

"You know. Oranges, bananas—"

"Doesn't seem enough."

"What do you mean?"

"Is that what you've been feeding Alexander?"

"He happens to love bananas mixed with rice cereal. Babies don't eat steak." Heat burned her cheeks. "Are you spying on me already? I thought you wanted to hear about Claire?"

"Go on," he said tersely.

Jann concentrated on the waves rolling in to the shore, remembering, never wanting to forget. "I was peeling my orange when a young woman came up that path from the beach. She seemed pale for someone with such dark hair." Jann glanced sideways at Peter. "Except for her paleness, she looked a lot like you."

The sun filtering through the Plumeria tree caught the line of Peter's jaw and the muscles rippling across it.

Jann hurried on, with difficulty wrenching her gaze from Peter's face. "She was out of breath, looked sick. I went to her." Jann swallowed hard. "I'll never forget her eyes. They were enormous . . . beautiful eyes." As her brother's eyes were beautiful, she thought, frowning back at Peter.

"I asked if she was all right and she told me she just needed to sit down for a moment, that she felt a bit dizzy. I took her arm and helped her to the bench."

"Was there nobody with her?"

"She didn't have any friends in Honolulu. She told me that later. Said she didn't need any, that she just wanted to be alone." Jann's throat clenched. "She seemed afraid, though, as if she didn't really mean it."

Abruptly, Peter stood, his movement creating a draft. Then his shadow fell over Jann, chilling her.

"She didn't have to be alone," he said tersely.

Jann stared up at him, tried to slow her suddenly rapid breathing. It was humiliating. She had spent years working to take control of her life and emotions, and in one fell swoop a stranger had turned everything upside down.

"I asked if she was sick and could I call someone for her," Jann went on, desperate to finish with this conversation. "Her face lit up as though someone had just handed her a present, and she told me, no, she wasn't sick. She laid her hand on her belly and said she was pregnant, that there was no one to call for the only person she cared about was right there inside her."

"Claire was wrong," Peter said fiercely, his face white and set. "She had me." He held out his hand again, the expression on his face demanding Jann take it.

The air surrounding her suddenly seemed stifling, as though all the oxygen had been siphoned away. His fingers captured hers and jerked her to her feet.

She lost her balance, for an instant, almost tumbling into his arms. Then he steadied her, his free hand touching her waist, but that was all it took for a current to surge between them.

# Chapter Three

First Peter's arm, then his hip, brushed against Jann as they walked together along the narrow beach path toward the marina. He held himself stiffly, not wanting to touch her again, for when he did, she drew him to her. He couldn't afford to be drawn. Not to a woman like her.

To anyone watching, they must seem an ordinary couple out for a morning stroll. But they were no ordinary couple. They weren't a couple at all.

"You must be hot in that jacket," Jann said, glancing at him sideways. She pulled a hankie from her pocket as though she were hot, too, and dabbed beads of perspiration off her forehead.

"I've been hotter," he said, trying to ignore the sweat inching up his spine, trying to ignore, as well, the reaction of his body to hers. Along his right side, where they almost touched, heat radiated as though he was next to a furnace.

She glanced at him again, eyebrows meeting in a frown.

"India, Africa, Asia," he said. "They're all hotter than Hawaii."

"That's right," she said, the crease between her eyes deepening. "Claire said you were always away."

The way she said it, it was a condemnation, and his fingers balled together in protest. He had been traveling in the tropics for what seemed like forever, but no matter how difficult, he'd always returned home regularly. To check in on Claire, to make sure she was all right.

To lay down the law was how Claire had seen it, that last terrible time they'd been together.

To keep her safe, he had countered, his gut tightening with fear when she'd slammed out of the house and driven down the drive at breakneck speed.

It was only with difficulty he'd stopped himself from going after her, remembering very clearly his own intensity at that age. At seventeen, she was neither grown up enough to have wisdom or young enough to accept advice graciously.

It had been different for him. He'd grown up in the month following his fourteenth birthday, when his careless mother had lost four year old Claire at a rock concert in the park.

He'd sworn that day, staring into his sister's tear-filled eyes, that he'd take care of her forever.

He'd done his best, but now she was dead.

"So Claire mentioned me?" he asked, wanting to think of his sister alive, not dead in some foreign soil.

"Sometimes."

Frowning, Peter glanced toward the street. "Shall we take my car or yours?"

"I don't have a car."

"What?" He stopped walking and turned to stare at her.

"Surely your fancy lawyer told you that?"

"No, he didn't," Peter said grimly. "How do you get around? More to the point, how does Alexander?"

"By bicycle."

"Bicycle!"

"You have heard of them?" she asked, her lips widening into a grin.

"That's no way to transport a baby. They're slow, dangerous—"

"Pollution free," she countered, "inexpensive and easy to park."

"But how do you carry Alexander?" Did she sling him in a knapsack and carry him on her back. He wouldn't put it past her. The woman had no practicality, no sense.

"In the usual way. In a little seat at the back."

"What if there's an emergency? What would you do then?"

"If he was ill, I'd call an ambulance." She cocked one brow skyward. "Wouldn't you?"

Terror flowed through Peter's veins at the thought of Alexander ill. He hadn't even met him yet, but already he loved him. He was Claire's. That was enough. "When you've got a baby to consider," he said, "you have to take every precaution, have to do things properly. I know the courts will feel the same."

Jann's smile died, and she swayed suddenly, her body wavering like a grass hut in a storm. With a muffled cry, she turned and ran down the path.

Jann's heart pounded so loudly, she could hear nothing else. She didn't know if Peter followed or if he was still standing there scowling. She only knew she had to get away, had to rid her head of all talk of courts. Rightly or wrongly, the courts had all the power. They could give, take away, even sometimes set you free. Or they could lock you behind stone walls so thick no sound could penetrate.

Footsteps sounded behind her and hard fingers grabbed her arm.

"What's the matter?" Peter growled as he whirled her around.

"Nothing," she lied, glaring into his eyes, realizing she had to face him. Fight him. Win!

"How far is it to your house?"

"I live over there." She extended her free arm and pointed, willing her hand to cease its shaking.

"Where?" he demanded irritably, staring across the water. "There's nothing there but boats."

"That's where I live," she said, shrugging her arm free. Turning, she continued on down the path.

His longer stride caught him up with her in seconds, his disapproval washing over her in near tangible waves.

Tightening her lips, she didn't look in his direction. Her boat was her home and she wouldn't have it any other way. Claire's brother could pack up his disapproval and take it back with him to Boston. As long as when he left, he didn't take Alex with him.

Her heart lurching at the thought, she pulled her sunglasses from her pocket and jammed them on her nose. In just a few minutes this man would scrutinize her home. She was damned if she was going to let him look into her soul as well.

"A boat's no place for a baby," he began, as soon as they stepped onto the pier.

"You're wrong," she disagreed softly. "Just stop for a moment and listen." Shutting her eyes, she did just that. Couldn't he feel it? Hear it? The slapping of the waves against the pilings. The movement of the pier. She opened her eyes again and stared straight into his. "It's soothing. Like being rocked in a cradle."

"He'll fall overboard."

"He's only six months old. He's not going to fall overboard."

"He'll be crawling soon."

"And I'll be watching him. Millions of people live on boats. You must know that from your travels."

"My nephew is not millions of people. But never mind," he said, shrugging, as though the tension tightening his shoulders had suddenly released, "by the time Alexander is crawling, he'll be back home with me in Boston."

Jann's palms grew damp. She turned left onto a smaller pier and hurried along it. Peter's footsteps echoed behind her, so loud, so . . . unbeatable.

She walked faster, needing now to feel the deck of her own boat beneath her feet, needing to know that below that deck Alex still safely slept.

Relief shafted through her at the sight of her sailboat's pale yellow bow poking out from between two white ones. Sunlight glinted off its smooth surface in rays filled with vitality and strength.

It had been six years since she had taken the money her parents had left her and made a down payment on the boat. Only two years more and *HEART'S DESIRE* would be completely hers.

A home of her own. Where no one could tell her it was time to move on, or force her to stay, either, locked behind metal mesh windows with other children who had no one to love them, surrounded by people who took care of them for money.

"Jann."

She stared blankly at Claire's brother, had almost forgotten he was there.

"Who's taking care of Alexander?" he demanded.

"My—"

"Thank God, you're back," a voice growled from the cockpit of Jann's boat. A bald-headed old man with a salt and pepper beard scrambled to a standing position and stepped nimbly across the narrow expanse of water from the deck to the pier. "And not soon enough!" he went on, his voice blustering down the dock toward them. "The little beggar's been howling all morning."

Peter turned an accusing gaze on her.

"Peter Strickland," Jann sighed, "meet John Miller."

"Call me Capt'n," the older man instructed, thrusting forward one gnarled hand, while his sharp gaze ranged curiously over the younger man's face. "You must be Alex's uncle. You're the spitting image of your sister."

Peter's body tensed.

"Nice little lassie, that one," Capt'n continued, his direct gaze daring anyone to disagree. He squeezed hard on

Peter's hand.

"Yes," Peter agreed.

"Got yourself a good grip there, laddie," the Capt'n said grudgingly, examining his fingers when he at last got them back.

"You must work out," Peter replied, giving him a smile.

Amazing how the smile warmed his face, Jann thought dazedly.

"Don't need to work out when you live an active life," Capt'n scoffed, puffing out his chest. "Lots of chores to do on a boat. Don't need those fancy gyms."

"Wouldn't have thought you'd have much time for babies," Peter remarked. "Do you have children of your own?"

"Never a one," the Capt'n replied, chuckling. "Don't know if that's a blessing or a curse."

"So how did you come to be the baby-sitter?" Peter asked.

Jann's chest tightened. He had almost fooled her for a moment into thinking he had another side, that he could be nice. But he was as tricky as a snake coiled to strike.

"She's got no one else, has she?" Capt'n replied, gesturing with a shaky finger towards Jann. "So she has to make do with—"

"Are you still here?" a high-pitched voice demanded, rising from the cabin of Jann's boat like a blast of hot steam. "You could have been to the store and back by now." Tanned fingers curled around the hatch, pushing it aside. A head emerged next, the tightly-curled hair attached to it wobbling indignantly.

"Oh, Lovey, it's you," the woman said, catching sight of Jann.

"Ruby Miller," Jann went on, feeling as a magician must when pulling a rabbit from a hat, "meet Claire's brother, Peter Strickland."

Her friend's smile cooled to a frown.

"Call me Peter," Claire's brother said, smiling politely at Ruby. Then he turned back to Jann, his expression unreadable. "We'll be seeing a lot of each other, after all."

She had seen too much already.

"Peter's here to meet Alex," Jann hastily explained.

"The little darling's asleep," Ruby said, the fine lines creasing her brow melting away. She slipped through the narrow hatchway and out onto the deck.

"Capt'n said he's given you a rough time this morning," Jann said worriedly.

"Now what made you say a thing like that?" Ruby demanded, glaring at her husband. "Men!" She rolled her eyes. "A little gas and they want to run for the hills. Alex only cried for a minute or two. As soon as he burped he was as right as rain."

Jann stepped aboard her boat and gave Ruby a grateful hug. "Thanks," she whispered into the older woman's ear.

"My pleasure," Ruby replied, holding her close a second longer. "I enjoy taking care of Alex and that's a fact. What time do you need us tomorrow?"

"I'm not sure yet. Could I pop down to the *WINDWARD* later and let you know?"

"That'll be fine, honey." She stepped onto the pier and touched her husband's arm. "Come along, old man, let's get home."

"Wait!" Jann cried, sudden panic twisting her gut. "You don't have to go yet!"

Her friends turned to her, looked startled.

"Stay and have a cup of tea," Jann suggested, her face growing hot.

"Not today, girl," Capt'n said, draping one arm around Ruby's shoulders. He started down the dock, moving Ruby along with him. "The two of you have things to discuss."

Slowly, reluctantly, Jann looked at Peter.

"May I come aboard?" he inquired, his voice studiously

polite.

"Of course," she agreed stiffly, wishing she could say no.

Two steps and he loomed above her, his outline framed by the noonday sun—powerful, urbane, and very, very masculine. Then he was in the cockpit with her and his bulk seemed to shrink the boat's size.

Putting out his hand, he lifted her sunglasses from her nose.

"Better," he pronounced, studying her eyes. "I can't see what you're thinking behind those things." His eyes glinted. "Or is that the idea?"

"The sun's strong in Hawaii," she said, willing away the further heat blazing her cheeks. "Better buy yourself a pair."

"I won't be here long enough for it to matter." He glanced impatiently toward the hatch. "Now where's Alexander? I want to see him."

"He's asleep. Why don't you come back tomorrow?"

"I will be back tomorrow, and the next day too."

The way he said it, it was a threat.

"But I'm not leaving here today without seeing my nephew." Then he looked around more slowly, making a visible effort to quell his impatience. "Nice little boat," he commented, reaching out to touch a stay.

The glow of pleasure his words brought unnerved Jann. This man was her enemy. If she cared what he thought, she'd be handing him power.

"Though no place for a child," he went on.

"It's thirty-seven feet!" Jann exclaimed, her glow fading as fast as it had bloomed. "I've seen families of four living on boats no larger."

"But not my nephew."

She sucked in a breath, tried to will herself to calmness. She would not let this man get to her, would not let him win.

"Would you like a cup of herbal tea?" she offered, forcing

her voice steady.

"A cup of coffee, if you've got it. Or . . ." He glanced at her hopefully. ". . . have you got anything cold?"

"Lemonade?" she offered, starting for the cabin door.

"Fine."

"I'll be back in a moment." She slipped down the companionway swiftly, not wanting him to accompany her. Better that he stay on deck and keep his cat's-eyes to himself!

A quick glance around the main cabin reassured her all was ship-shape. Alex's things, especially, had a habit of spreading across a room like barnacles on a ship's hull. With a sigh of relief she moved into the tiny galley, opened the refrigerator door, and groped at the back for the jug of lemonade.

"Need any help?"

Jerking back her hand, Jann whirled around.

Peter's long, lean form dwarfed the inside of her cabin as thoroughly as it had the cockpit. He stood by the companionway, toying with the heart-shaped paperweight he must have picked up from her desk.

"No," she gulped, watching uneasily as his gaze drifted around the cabin, pausing first on her collection of glazed pottery bowls, whose scarlet color and heart shapes made them pulse with life, then moving on to the miniature, heart-shaped clock her grandmother had given her on her sixth birthday. To celebrate learning to tell the time, her granny had said.

It felt, at this moment, as though time had stopped.

"You must believe in love," Peter said, looking next at the heart-shaped twig wreath Ruby had given her last Christmas.

"Not particularly," she replied, "though some people manage it." Her parents had. Capt'n and Ruby, too.

But it wasn't for her.

"Do you believe in it?" she asked.

Ignoring her question, he turned his attention to the

framed photographs papering one wall of the cabin.

Jann's shoulders tensed. She'd won an award for the first picture, a photo of a homeless woman squinting up into the afternoon sun. But next to it were photos of Alex. Pictures she'd prefer this man not see. She'd captured her baby's innocence in all his moods, whether crying or smiling or staring solemnly around with his old man's eyes. When Peter reached them, she ceased to breathe.

He slowly reached for the photo in the middle, the one of Claire, her face glistening with perspiration and joy as she held out her arms for Alex the very first time.

"Who took this?" Peter demanded softly, taking hold of the frame with knuckle-whitened fingers and lifting the photo from its hook.

"I did," Jann said, the sheer unfairness of Claire's death, as always, overwhelming her.

"All of them?" His sharp gaze swept the walls.

"Yes."

"Who taught you to take pictures like these?" He looked at her then in a clear, glittering glance, before shifting his attention to the wall beside her where hung a photo of an aged Hawaiian woman gazing off into the distance, her face creased into a multitude of wrinkles. Her husband stood behind her, one hand resting on her shoulder in a timeless gesture of solidarity and love.

"Nobody, exactly," Jann said, but she remembered her father at his easel, his brush strokes capturing the precise curve of her mother's smile. She had inherited her father's eye, a gift that had come as swiftly and as unexpectedly as her parents had gone.

She turned back to the refrigerator and reached again for the lemonade. Her hand trembled and she spilled a few drops on her tiny countertop.

"It's just something I do," she explained quietly. Something she couldn't stop doing if she tried. "My job." More than a job, her sanity.

"They're good."

With reluctance, she met his eyes, trying again not to care that he liked them. If she worried what people thought, her gift would disappear, and with it, she believed, the stark honesty of her photos.

Peter turned his attention back to the picture in his hand.

"Keep it," Jann offered, the words escaping her lips before she realized they were there.

"I'll buy it," he said in return.

"It's not for sale."

His jaw clenched. With deliberate care he placed the photo back on its nail, then slowly turned to face her.

"Where's my nephew?" he demanded.

"Why? So you can buy him, too?"

"I want to see him."

"Once you've seen him, I want you to leave."

She pushed past Peter, past his solid, statue-like immovability, and moved swiftly down the passage toward Alex's cabin. Before she opened his door, she pulled in a deep, cleansing breath, not want-ing even a hint of the tension swirling through her boat to enter her baby's room. Since Clare had died, she'd done everything she could to wrap Alex in love, and she was not about to let Peter Strickland's possessiveness seep in and destroy that love.

Her baby slept peacefully, his face rosy in the glow of the sun sparkling through the glass hatch. His black hair, flattened by sleep, clung softly to the edges of his face.

Fear slivered through Jann. If Claire's brother gained custody of Alex, how would she survive?

"He looks like Claire."

She hadn't heard Peter approaching. Incredibly, she hadn't sensed him, but now she knew he was near, her nerve-endings jangled loudly enough to wake the dead.

He leaned over her shoulder, his breath tickling the hairs on the back of her neck. She could smell him again, a clean scent overlaid with the subtle bouquet of his aftershave. Turning, she faced him, placing her body solidly between his and that of her child.

Desire raged through her, sharp and unexpected, loosening her limbs and softening her lips.

Peter seemed to feel it also, for his eyes widened with shock, and gazed into her own so intently her breathing stopped. His eyes changed color from sea-green to emerald and for one agonizing instant, she was sure he meant to kiss her. Was sure, too, that the idea appalled him as much as it did her.

With a swift intake of breath, she scooped up her sleeping son and thrust him towards his uncle. Alex awoke, his face wrinkling with outrage, and his mouth opened wide in a high-pitched baby cry.

For a single second only, Jann felt safe, an obstacle now between her and this man who could destroy her life. Then her lips parted in a soundless protest, for Alex, beloved Alex, was in the hands of the man who could take him from her.

With a gentle motion, Peter turned the small bundle to face him, his gaze softening as he stared down at his sister's child. A man like him, so large and strong, should appear awkward holding a baby, but this man didn't. He held Alexander as though he had been doing it forever.

A lump formed in Jann's throat, making it impossible to swallow.

Peter stroked Alex's cheek and the baby's howls died to nothing. Solemnly reaching into his jacket pocket, Peter pulled out a tattered, ear-chewed-off teddy bear.

"This is for you, Alexander Strickland," he said, speaking to his nephew so softly, Jann had to strain to hear. "It was your mother's."

# Chapter Four

Jann tugged her hair back from her face and looped it into a knot on the top of her head before stepping over the railing on the stern of her boat. Standing on the lip of the deck, she reached back and up as far as she could. No good. She was tall, but not tall enough.

Cautiously, she lifted first one leg then the other back over the railing until she was sitting on it, the pole of the wind generator between her legs. By stretching hard, the ends of her fingers brushed the release button of the telescoping pole. But she couldn't push it in. The sea air and ocean spray had corroded and stiffened the metal.

With a sigh, she slumped forward against the pole. Alex grinned toothlessly up at her from the high chair she had jammed against the back corner of the cockpit, and clapped his hands together, as though cheering her efforts. She smiled back at him, then, the smile turning to a frown, returned her gaze to the wind generator high above her head.

She needed it in working order for her trip to Maui next week, but couldn't seem to fix it, was too tired to make the extra effort. And that was Peter Strickland's fault. She'd lain awake half the night, unable to forget how out of control she'd felt when they'd almost kissed.

"Damn." Capt'n's growl carried easily from his boat to Jann's.

"What are you doing out there?" Ruby demanded irritably, her voice still filled with sleep. "John, you're not working on that rudder again! You promised to hire someone to help you."

Jann chuckled. The Capt'n might be a mechanical genius but even working a lifetime as ship's engineer on a large freighter in the South Pacific hadn't prepared him for the idiosyncrasies of the run-down old sloop he and Ruby had bought when they retired last year.

An indistinct murmur grabbed Jann's attention. Peering toward the WINDWARD through a forest of intervening masts, she saw no one. But she didn't need to see Peter Strickland to recognize his voice.

"Need some help?"

Capt'n wouldn't want any help from Peter.

"Much obliged," Capt'n answered gruffly.

Frowning, Jann clutched the pole more tightly and leaned sideways until she could make out the WINDWARD's bow. It rocked up as Peter stepped onto the stern.

"Can't seem to make the darn thing work right," Capt'n complained querulously.

"Maybe, if you . . . ."

The rest was lost in a series of thumps and bangs.

"By God, that did the trick!" Capt'n exclaimed, when the noise suddenly died. "How about a cup of coffee?"

Now he was serving Peter coffee!

The boat rocked again as the two men moved forward.

"What an unusual carving," Peter said, his voice now sharp and clear. "Not from around here, is it?"

She could imagine Claire's brother staring, his green eyes narrowed, at the painted wooden mask Capt'n kept nailed to the front of the cabin. Her frown deepened.

"Picked it up in New Guinea on my last voyage there," Capt'n explained.

"I have one just like it," Peter said thoughtfully. "Got it from a fellow in Port Moresby—Jeff Andrews, his name was."

"Jeff! You know Jeff? Ruby, did you hear that? He knows Jeff."

Now they had mutual friends. Jann rested her cheek against the pole, her stomach lurching queasily. She clung there, staring at the mast on the boat opposite, hoping a focal point would rid her body of the dizziness overtaking her.

". . . no, I won't have more coffee, thanks. I need to talk to Jann."

Short of casting off and putting out to sea there was no avenue of escape, Jann decided. Damn the man. She had work to do. Pressing her lips together, she stretched again toward the stubborn button, concentrating on that, ignoring the sound of Peter's feet padding closer along the pier.

"Good morning," he said.

"What do you want?" she muttered, uncomfortably aware of her too-short cut-offs and skimpy, clinging tee shirt.

"You know why I'm here."

Reluctantly, she lowered her arms. Today he was dressed for the heat. Two strongly-muscled, tanned legs stretched up then disappeared beneath a pair of khaki shorts. A rust-colored tee shirt lay snug across his broad chest and his green eyes were focused on her. She dragged the back of her hand across her brow, wiping away the moisture forming there.

"I told you before you left last night that you couldn't see Alex until this evening. I'll be on a shoot all day." She'd been looking forward all week to the shoot at Sunset Beach. Now she was probably too exhausted to do her work properly.

"I'm here to baby-sit," he said evenly, waggling his fingers at Alex.

Her baby chortled back at him and the finger of toast he was attempting to maneuver into his mouth slipped from between chubby fingers and landed on the deck. Alex's smile crumpled into an O-shaped wail.

"Ruby and Capt'n are baby-sitting," Jann said firmly.

"I'll help," Peter said, then stepping on board, he retrieved Alex's toast and handed it back to the baby.

"No! Your visits have to be supervised."

"John and Ruby will supervise."

"I have to supervise."  Her fingers tightened around the pole.

"Then you don't leave me much choice."

"What do you mean?"

"Alexander and I will go with you."

"You can't!" From the hardening line of his jaw, Jann saw he not only could, but would. "It'll be too hard on Alex—that long bus ride, no place to nap—"

"I have a car," he reminded her implacably. "With a baby seat."

"I might not even go," she muttered.

"Why not?"

"Got to fix this first." She gestured with a grimace toward the metal pole.

"What is it?"

"A wind generator."

"How do you expect to work on it from there?"

"The pole telescopes down. I just have to release this darned button."

"Let me have a look." He edged around Alex's high chair and stepped closer.

"I can do it."

"You're going to fall overboard the way you're sitting."

"I never have yet!"

"Are you going to move?" he demanded, suddenly closer than she wanted him, almost as close as they'd been last night.

"No," she snapped. He was the one who needed to move. She couldn't work with him this close, couldn't think. Tearing her gaze away from his ocean-colored eyes, she stretched upward toward the button.

"You'll never reach it," he insisted, and without waiting for her assent, grabbed hold of the pole to which she clung and swung his legs over the railing.

Placing his feet on the lip of the deck, he moved around behind her, his body now snug against her back and bottom, with one arm looped around her body as his hand grasped the pole. Then he stretched in the same direction as she, and his hand met hers.

She gasped at the current coursing between their fingers, the connection as electric as the heat flaming the flesh of her back. His breath was on her neck, sweet breath, and warm, making her long to kiss him and to be kissed in return.

"Get off me," she cried, fighting the sudden desire to turn in his arms.

He stiffened, but he, too, must have felt the heat, for when she twisted around to face him, desire blazed in his eyes.

"I've almost got it," he muttered, his jaw tightening stubbornly. He stretched higher, his body rubbing against hers with the movement, inflaming her even further.

"I said get off." Her panic rose. To sink into his heat was as impossible as it was desirable. She pushed against him, fearing to lose herself in his touch.

With a garbled shout, and a sudden wrenching of heat from heat, he was gone, the splash his body made as it entered the water drenching her.

Stunned by his sudden fall, she swung her legs off the railing and stood where he had stood, one hand clutching the pole, the other shading her eyes. She struggled to pick out his shape hidden in the shadows on the water's surface.

"Peter!" she shouted, her heart pounding so hard it reverberated against her eardrums.

"John! Ruby! Help!" she screamed.

Only a ripple showed where the surface had been disturbed. Save for that ripple and the heat still coursing through her, there was no evidence Peter had ever been there. She counted to ten, then with a swift glance to see that Alex was safely strapped in his highchair, she dove into the salty water.

Her open eyes stung from the shock of it, but she couldn't see Peter, could see nothing but shadows.

She dove deeper, her hands stretched out before her, glad

now for little clothing and no shoes to slow her down. Then a darker shadow floated near from the buoy on her left and she could see it was Peter.

She reached for him, thinking to catch hold of his arm and pull him to the surface, but his hand shot out and grasped her wrist instead. Despite the cold water, his fingers burned. With a sharp tug, he very quickly had her skimming upwards.

"What the hell did you think you were doing?" he demanded, the moment their heads broke the surface. He glared at her, his eyes dark and fierce.

"Are you hurt?" she asked.

"No," he yelled. "No thanks to you!"

"You were crowding me!" Even here, in the middle of the ocean, he was crowding her. He shook his head to clear wet black hair from his eyes and water sprayed over her. His legs tangled with hers as they paddled to keep afloat.

"I was helping you," he growled.

"I didn't need any help."

"So you thought you'd dump me overboard?"

"Next time maybe you'll listen."

"Is that what you intend to do to Alexander if he doesn't do what you tell him? Push him overboard?"

"No, I . . ." She bit her lip.

"And what do you mean jumping in after me and leaving Alexander alone?"

She shot a swift glance toward her boat. She couldn't see Alex from where she floated but she could hear his happy babbling.

"Alex is fine," she said firmly.

"Funny place for a swim," John called from above, peering over the side of Jann's boat and grinning down at them.

"Just cooling off," Peter said grimly.

"It was hot," Jann said evasively, then looked toward Peter and saw his eyes weren't as angry as they'd been before. In fact, if she didn't know better, she could have sworn there was laughter lurking in their depths.

"Let's get out," Peter said, giving her arm a gentle tug. His lips stretched into a full-fledged grin. "I've had enough swimming for one day."

"Isn't summer off-season for the big surf?" Peter asked, pulling back his arm, then casting a pebble far out into the oncoming breakers.

"Yes," she answered, struggling to keep her voice matter-of-fact while screwing the telephoto lens onto her camera. "There's been some bad weather around the islands lately." She stared past Peter to the ocean. "Unusual for this time of year."

"Hand me that film, would you?" she asked, glancing back at him and holding out her hand. He touched her palm as he gave it to her, his fingers scoring her skin with warmth.

"Thanks," she said swiftly, snatching her hand away.

"It's been interesting," he said.

"What has?" Jann asked. "The beach?" She fit the film into its slot before looking at him again.

"Watching you work," he replied, with a lazy smile.

"I'm supposed to be supervising you," she said, uncomfortably aware at how easily his smile warmed her, "not the other way around."

"I thought we agreed to keep an eye on each other."

"I didn't agree to anything." Heat spread up her neck, and she was irritated anew at her inability to forget how his skin felt on hers.

Claire had said her brother was clever and controlling. He was also trying to take Alex away. She'd be a fool to forget that.

Jann glanced down the broad sweep of beach glistening in the sunlight. The surf, as usual, pulled her gaze.

"The Bonsai Pipeline," she said slowly, determined to put

Peter into a different place, to make him into something he wasn't. A tourist, nothing more. "It lures surfers from all over the world. A God to some. To others . . ." She stared at the enormous breakers and couldn't stop a shiver from skittering across her shoulders. ". . . a killer."

Then she raised her camera to her eye and scanned the water, finding, at long last, the surfer she'd been watching most of the afternoon.

The young man's face was contorted with the effort of concentration as he lay on his board paddling furiously before a gigantic wave. At just the right moment he scrambled to his feet, then, his body bending like a sapling in the wind, he balanced on the wave's crest and clung to the crashing water.

Again and again, Jann pressed the camera's shutter, excitement buoying her up as she caught the very moment the surfer knew he was there, that with skill and good luck the wave would be his. She caught, too, his exultation.

"Did you get it?" Peter asked, his voice carrying the same excitement Jann felt inside and coming from somewhere close to her ear.

"Yes," she cried happily, forgetting to be wary. "I got exactly what I wanted."

He grinned down at her, his hair blowing in the wind. Jann's heart began pounding like an out-of-control drum, then lurched suddenly to a halt. Impulsively, inexplicably, she raised her camera to her eye and pressed down on the shutter.

A soundproof wall seemed to descend around her, the noise of the surf disappearing, as did the laughter of the people walking by on the sand. All that remained was the slow thumping of her heart, suddenly and erratically, resuming its beat. She stood motionless, her cheeks on fire, unwilling to lower the camera and face him.

With an inward moan, slowly and reluctantly, she did just that. Peter's full lips had curved into a smile and one brow was questioningly raised.

She glanced down to where her baby lay sleeping on a blanket. "I thought Alex should have something to remember you by when you leave," she said defiantly, grateful to the child for the excuse coming to mind.

Peter laughed, a full-bodied, heart-stopping explosion of sound that erupted from his chest and made mincemeat of her lies. Then he slowly leaned towards her, placing one hand on the back of her head as his lips descended to hers.

The first touch of their warmth drifted somewhere between a promise and a threat, pummeling her with the power of the sea, demanding . . . enticing . . . relentless. Hard lips, yet smooth as satin, and salty from the ocean air.

Desire, as unbidden as the kiss, snaked through Jann's body and molded her lips to his. Another moan, as soft as a sigh this time, rolled up from her throat. Twisting her head away, she stepped backward, chest heaving. Tendrils of her hair, snatched by the wind from the elastic tie holding them, whipped against her face like harsh threads of reality.

Peter's smile died. "I shouldn't have done that," he said quietly, his stunned expression revealing to her the shock the kiss had given him.

"No," Jann whispered back. "Why did you?"

"Just something for you to remember me by when Alex and I leave."

The world seemed to swirl, flipping end-over-end like a leaf in the wind. Desperate for an anchor, Jann forced her gaze downward to the pink-tinged cheeks of her sleeping baby.

Until Alex had come along, she had kept everyone steadfastly locked from her heart. But she'd let Alex in and now she had to keep him safe. Had to keep him with her.

"I want to go now," she said.

"Alexander is sleeping," Peter countered, in a voice as strained as her own. "Don't wake him."

She was tempted to do just that, willing to do anything necessary to get away from this place and away from this man who was winning her baby over. But with Alex sleeping so peacefully, she couldn't bring herself to do it.

She risked a glance at Peter and found him watching her, his expression showing no sign now of the dark emotion just moments before. Stifling a sigh, she put her camera in its bag and set it on a log.

An off-shore breeze fluttered the edges of the lamb skin she'd tucked around Alex. She slipped down beside him, determined to leave the second he awoke.

Peter moved back to the water's edge and stood there a moment as motionless as a statue staring out at the ocean.

Was he thinking about Alex? Jann envied him his tie by blood to the most important person in her world.

Then she saw his hand clench. He couldn't be thinking of Alex. Not if he was angry. He must be thinking of her and the kiss they had shared. Regretting it.

One thing she could be sure of, he wasn't thinking about Claire. Jann angrily scrubbed away a tear. According to her friend, in the year-and-a-half since Claire left high school, Peter had vetoed everything she wanted to do, had distrusted her, and investigated her friends. Claire had hated that.

Suddenly, Peter faced her, the sun now low on the horizon behind him, making it impossible to read what was in his eyes. Stepping forward, he lowered himself to the blanket.

Catching her breath and holding it, Jann willed her body small. For if he touched her again, she would tumble into his warmth, and that was not a sensation she could afford to repeat.

Then his shoulder brushed hers and, as spine-tingling as an electric current, the hairs on her arm sprang up.

"Besides," Peter continued softly, as though he had never ceased their conversation, as though he had never kissed her, "the sun will be setting in a few minutes. We don't want to miss that."

Sunset.

Magic—shared with the right person.

But she'd never had and couldn't afford to want a person like that in her life, for love wasn't worth the pain that was sure to follow.

She drew herself up stiffly. "Alex will be awake before sunset."

"Then he'll enjoy it with us."

She stole a glance sideways. The light of the lowering sun reflected off Peter's eyes, concealing all expression, filling them with mystery.

"Besides," he added, smiling at her faintly, "I didn't come all the way to Sunset Beach to miss the sunset."

A knot formed in Jann's stomach, and she turned away, but she sensed before she actually felt his fingers gripping her chin.

"Forget the kiss," he ordered, gently turning her head to face him. "Concentrate on the sunset."

How could she concentrate on anything when her jaw trembled against the rough-smooth texture of his fingers?

"Cold?" he murmured. Not waiting for her reply, he pulled off his sweater and laid it across her shoulders.

It hung heavy, weighing her down, the warmth of his body still captured within. It heated her throughout, but was in some way too familiar, as though Peter himself was the one who held her. Easing the sweater off, she let it drop to the blanket. If Peter noticed her action, he didn't let on.

"Look," he whispered instead, pointing out to sea.

The sun was a ball of flame, flung as if by some giant to the distant horizon, while overhead the sky was pink, deepening to magenta in places, then to violet, even purple, tone layering tone in a cacophony of color.

Peter sprawled lower, seeming as relaxed beside her as she was tense. If she could simply ignore him, not look at him. Blinking hard, she reached for her camera, screwed on a wide-angled lens, and focused it on the skyline.

Without warning, his fingers covered hers, sending a tingling sensation exploding up her arm.

"Don't hide behind that camera, Jann."

"I'm not," she protested hoarsely.

"That's a lie." Gently, insistently, he pulled on her hand, forcing the camera away from her face. "You're afraid of something," he accused softly, staring intently into her eyes. "I know you are. I can feel it."

Fear shafted through her.

"I'll find out," he promised, "whatever it is." He glanced up at the sky, his gaze now holding the same fire as the heaven's light. "Besides," he went on, "you can't capture a sunset with photographs."

"What do you mean?" she stammered.

"Look at it."

Easier to look at the sky than to look at Peter. She couldn't risk that with this inexplicable heat invading her body.

"Within seconds," Peter said, "it'll be different. If you look away, you'll miss it." He sounded as certain of this as though it had happened to him.

The sky was immense and they were nothing, yet it felt as though the man beside her had woven a spell around the three of them, had turned their blanket into a haven. As if they belonged together, and were one with the oncoming night.

But that was false. She couldn't let him in or he would rip her world apart.

Only Alex belonged with her, and she with him.

Somewhere down the beach a ukulele tinkled. Then another. And another. Hawaiian voices, so sweet Jann's throat ached, rose up in song.

The notes soared, then fell, then soared again, twisting and twining in a rhythm as ancient as time, singing a farewell to this day and a blessing on the next.

Jann took hold of Alex's hand and gently stroked his palm. Even in his sleep, his fingers grasped hers with the instinct of the newborn.

Her hand tightened protectively around his smaller one. She had promised Claire she would care for Alex and she wasn't about to break that promise. Peter didn't love this child as she did and all the money and security in the world couldn't make up for that.

"It's like a promise."

She looked at Peter, stunned. "What do you mean?" Was he reading her mind again?

"When the sky looks like that . . ."

But he wasn't looking at the sky now. He was looking at her. She could drown in eyes like his as easily as in the ocean.

". . . it's as though the pain you feel today is over and will never come back. It almost makes you believe in promises."

Her pulse faded to nothing. "I've always believed in promises." She stared into his eyes as deeply as she dared. "Especially the ones I make."

# Chapter Five

Jann's head sank lower and lower until her chin brushed the top of her handlebars. Her legs pumped rapidly, her thigh muscles screaming for relief. Sweat dripped from her face and she could barely feel the pressure of the pedals on her feet, they spun so rapidly around the shaft.

It felt good when she could move like this, streaking along as fast as her muscles would allow. She could forget about Peter Strickland then and the knot now permanently lodged in her stomach.

There was a man sitting on Claire's bench.

Her fingers tightened convulsively on her handbrakes and the bike stopped so suddenly she had to lower her feet to steady herself.

It was Peter. There was no escaping him. He was everywhere; on her boat, in her thoughts, in the shape of Alex's eyes . . . and now here.

But he hadn't seen her yet. Maybe she could simply head back to the boat. Maybe . . . . No, he'd be there shortly anyway, as he had been every morning for the past six days, every morning since their trip to Sunset Beach.

Filling Jann with fear. For Alex had become more and more enamored of his uncle as each day passed, judging Peter by some curious baby standard and finding him perfect.

She slowly placed her feet back on the pedals. If Peter's intention was to wear her down, he was succeeding.

She pedaled closer, was almost upon him before he looked up. She stifled a gasp. Peter's skin seemed too tight for his face and his lips were a mere line in his face. For one long endless moment, he simply stared at her, his eyes blank and unseeing. Then, as though mustering the determination from somewhere deep within, he rearranged his features into a tight-lipped smile.

Resting her feet uncertainly on either side of her bicycle, Jann remained where she was, fighting again the overwhelming inclination to flee.

That he was in pain was obvious. What she should do about it, she didn't know.

"What are you doing here?" Peter asked.

"I ride by here every day," Jann mumbled, slowly getting off her bike and laying it down on the grass. She moved toward the bench and sat down.

"That's right," he said bitterly, "this is where you met Claire."

"Yes," Jann answered softly, touched by the grief written on his face. "Were you thinking about her just now?"

He didn't answer, but his eyes were bright, too bright. Then even as she watched, that trace of vulnerability disappeared.

"Were you with her when she died?" he asked.

The nightmare of Claire's death flooded straight from Jann's heart to her brain. Her face drained of heat and Peter's face looked every bit as bad. His eyes burned like two lanterns in the night, locking her gaze to his and refusing to let go.

"Tell me what happened," he demanded hoarsely.

Sympathy surged through her. It seemed to have cost Peter everything to ask, as it had cost her everything to watch.

"Just days after Alex was born," Jann began, hugging herself with her arms, her body suddenly chilled, "Claire got a headache." More than a mere headache. It had been as if her friend's head had been put in a vise and squeezed.

"I stayed with her at her apartment to help with Alex," Jann continued, not wanting to remember, but unable to forget. "I wanted to call the doctor, but Claire refused to let me. She insisted it was only a touch of the flu. Said she'd had enough of doctors during her pregnancy."

"She never liked going to the doctor," Peter said tonelessly.

"Even as a child."

"Her headache got worse. By the third day, she couldn't even get out of bed. She still refused to see the doctor, seemed afraid of what he'd say." Helplessness flooded over Jann, as sharp now as it had been the day Claire died.

"You should have made her go," Peter accused.

"I know that now," Jann said miserably, rubbing one hand along her icy arm. "In the end, I called Ruby and the Capt'n. Ruby was a nurse before she and the Capt'n retired. They stayed with the baby and I was able to convince Claire to come with me to the hospital." She stopped, unable for a moment to go on. "But I should have called the doctor sooner." She lowered her gaze. "I was afraid."

Peter grasped her arm. She stared at the place where his hand burned her skin, his fingers like rings of fire while the rest of her froze.

"The doctor examined Claire," she finally continued, her lips barely moving, "then they whisked her away." She looked again at Peter, praying he would understand.

"They wouldn't let me see her or tell me anything about her condition for hours," Jann went on, her throat thickening, her words dying. It had been the same when her parents had been in the hospital.

"Tell me the rest of it," Peter commanded, still holding onto her arm, seeming intent on wrenching the story from her by force if he had to.

But there was no need to force anything. If he wanted this story, he could have it. She wanted only to forget. Maybe once it was out, she would. Swallowing hard, she tried again.

"When they let me in to see her, I . . . I'd never seen anyone look so pale." Certainly not Claire, with her brown skin and brilliant eyes. Like Alex's eyes. And Peter's.

She'd been reluctant at first to speak, but now the words wouldn't stop. "They said Claire had a blood clot in the brain.

They wouldn't say how she got it." Jann's voice faded. "I guess they didn't know."

"What did they do for her?" Peter asked fiercely.

"They couldn't do anything. The clot was in an impossible location. They couldn't operate. We could only pray it wouldn't move." She bleakly met Peter's gaze. "But it did."

With a suddenness that stunned, he let go of her arm. Staring down at where his fingers had been, Jann felt inexplicably bereft.

"Then what happened?" he asked softly, staring at the ocean now, sitting so still he seemed scarcely alive.

"Nothing right away. Claire lived for a couple more days after the doctors diagnosed what was wrong. They gave her medicine for her pain." Staring at Peter's profile, Jann wished her words could be different. "The pain in her head, that is. There was nothing they could do about the pain in her heart."

Muscles twitched along Peter's jaw line, but he made no other movement.

"What about Alex?" he finally asked.

Tears welled in Jann's eyes. "I brought him in every day to see his mother. Ruby came too, so that she could take Alex home again while I stayed with Claire. She tried to be cheerful while Alex was with her. She was so brave."

"Claire was always brave."

"But sometimes . . . when I caught her unawares, her face was . . ." Jann took hold of the bench armrest, clinging to what was left of her swiftly-fleeing control. "When I came home to Alex at night," she continued, starting in a different place, "I would hold him. I told myself it was for him, but . . ." She gave a helpless shrug. "I guess I needed his hugs as much as he did mine."

"And then?" Peter faced her again, seemed to steel himself to bear the truth.

She lifted her hands, then let them fall into her lap with a thud. "Claire died," she whispered.

The silence following her words seemed to last an eternity.

"Were you with her?" he finally asked, as he had asked once before, but this time his voice rasped like a file over metal.

"Yes." A single tear trickled down Jann's cheek. Then as though a dam had broken, the trickle turned into a flood.

The sob erupting from her breast had to be coming from someone else. She didn't cry. Not anymore. But one sob followed another, until she couldn't breathe, couldn't think. All she could do was feel, and the feeling was one great blanket of pain.

Dimly, she felt Peter take hold of her shoulders and pull her towards him, until she sank against his body like a ship at anchor, powerless to stop swaying with the tide.

His breath warmed her cheek and his arms warmed her body, holding her safe within their circle. Human warmth, warmth of the living. Somehow it managed to push back the agony she'd been fighting since the night her friend had died, pushed back her dread that Alex would be next just because she loved him.

As she had loved Claire. And her own parents.

The warmth moved inward through her skin until it touched her soul, until for one glorious moment she felt at peace.

She sat as still as she was able, for if she moved, the spell might vanish. Peter's heart thumped against her cheek, the sound of it loud, so reassuringly there. It seemed incredible that this man, whom she'd thought so dangerous, was so undeniably safe.

She lifted her head and looked at him, the slight stubble on his chin grazing her forehead. A strong chin. As he was strong. A tremor went through her that he seemed to feel, also, for he looked down at her then and the expression in his eyes softened.

At the sight of Peter's lips, so warm, full and close, her own lips parted. For an instant only, his lips touched hers, long enough to comfort, and then deny.

Sucking in a ragged breath, Jann pulled away.

He straightened, also, seeming to turn inward, away from her, separate.

After a very long moment he spoke to her again. "Why didn't you notify me when Claire was taken ill," he asked, his voice cracking as though from disuse.

Jann shivered, feeling as bad again now as she had before. She had intended to phone Boston, to contact the scratched-out number she could barely distinguish in Claire's address book.

But Claire had said no, had in fact screamed it, long and frighteningly. Jann and Ruby had stared at each other help-lessly, amazed at Claire's vocal and insistent refusal to contact her brother. And at the time, it hadn't seemed to matter. They had never imagined that three days later, Claire would be dead.

It mattered now.

"Claire didn't want us to," Jann explained, the words sounding ridiculous, the pain in Peter's eyes rubbing her heart to the quick.

"Didn't want you to?" he demanded incredulously. "Surely she was past knowing what she wanted?"

"No, she wasn't. She was very definite."

"What explanation did she give?"

Jann hesitated. To repeat Claire's words seemed impossible somehow.

"Claire said no one really cared," she began reluctantly, "that all her aunt and uncle were concerned about was money and power. She'd been living with them since she was ten, since . . ." Jann looked away from Peter again, tried to soften her words. ". . . since your parents died."

"I know where she'd been living," he said impatiently.

"Then you should have known how unhappy she was."

This woman was right, Peter thought guiltily. He should have known.

"She had everything she needed," he went on slowly, thinking back to the list that had been recited to him, "a home, friends, family." But he had been Claire's closest family. He should have been there when she needed him the most.

"She had a house," Jann countered. "That was all. There was no warmth there. Her so-called family didn't bother with her other than to see that she was fed and clothed. They simply wanted her to do what she was told and not make a fuss."

Peter closed his eyes, wishing he could as easily shut out Jann's barrage of words. His father had often told them they were never to make a fuss. Which was why when their mother neglected them, he had never spoken up. Perhaps if he had . . .

"Your aunt and uncle didn't care if she was happy," Jann went on hotly, "or make any effort to see that she was. They even dismissed her nanny. Said she was too old to be clinging to what was over."

"She was too old," Peter said dully. Although he'd tried to protect his sister from the worst of their mother's excesses, they'd both been thrust into maturity before their time. "She started boarding school that year."

"Yes, but don't you see? She didn't have anyone."

This woman who seemed able to look straight into his soul was staring into his eyes again as though searching for the truth.

"Not even you," she finished.

"I was there," Peter protested, but he hadn't been able to convince Claire of that. "She could have talked to me."

"She tried." Jann's eyes welled with tears. "She said you didn't care. That's what hurt her the most."

"I did care," Peter said fiercely. "But I was at school too. I came back from England at every break in that first year after our parents died. I told Claire that as soon as I finished at Cambridge, we could be together at Willow House just as she wanted."

"But that never happened! You never came for her."

Fury swept over him again as it had done so long ago. "I did come," he said tightly, "but she wasn't there. My aunt and uncle had already enrolled her in boarding school."

"So you left it at that?"

Jann's face mirrored her feelings, the pain evident in her eyes. And her lips trembled, as though she knew only too well what it was like to have no one.

"They said it was ridiculous to imagine I could take care of her myself," he explained bitterly. "And sitting there in their plush sitting room, with maids trotting to and fro, it did seem ridiculous. What did I know about taking care of a young girl?"

"Besides," he went on, hating the emotion rising in his chest, "they told me she was happy, that she'd just started school, that if she were disrupted again, the consequences could be grave." He swallowed hard. "They seemed so certain." As positive about everything as he had been unsure.

Jann stretched her hand towards him, as though she guessed what he was feeling and was somehow sorry. He stiffened and leaned away.

"I didn't have to explain this to you," he said, standing. "It won't matter a damn in a court of law. But I did explain, so you'd know. Maybe now, you'll understand how wrong Claire was and stop this ridiculous clinging to Alexander."

"It's you who doesn't understand," Jann countered sharply, "about both Claire and Alex. Claire didn't trust you before, and I don't now."

"I wrote to Claire from Cambridge, and she wrote back.

She didn't say anything in her letters about being unhappy." Though he'd worried at the time she might be keeping her unhappiness hidden.

"She complained about the school food," he went on, trying to smile. "I told her about my business plans, how we could spend more time together once she finished school. But she didn't reply."

"She was probably afraid to get her hopes up."

"What are you afraid of, Jann?" he asked her softly, stunned that he'd asked the question. He couldn't afford to become embroiled in this woman's pains or dreams. If he had to fight her, he must remain aloof.

She straightened her shoulders, as though bracing herself to reply, all the while looking at him as though he were a shark, poised and ready to strike.

"Nothing," she replied, giving her hair a determined toss. "This isn't about me."

"That's exactly what this is about." He willed his heart to harden against her, not melt at her deceptive warmth. "You're like all the others."

"What others?"

"Claire was always wanting to spend her trust money on one lame duck or other, said they'd do well if they could only get on their feet." He scowled at Jann, forcing himself to remember those other times he now wanted to forget. "Those so-called friends used my sister."

She looked as though she'd been slapped, and again he stifled the impulse to reach for her, to hold her close.

"Claire said you turned Alex's father over to the police," Jann said harshly, as though she didn't care how that made him feel.

"He was a drug dealer," Peter explained, "a user and a pusher. He would have taken everything Claire had; her money, trust and innocence . . . then he would have destroyed her."

"Claire said you did that."

"She was wrong," he said flatly. "Alexander's father died before he even got to prison. Of a drug overdose." He stared hard at Jann, willing her to understand. "Is that what you would have wanted for Claire?"

"No," the woman opposite whispered, and she shivered suddenly, as though Claire's sorrow was around her as much as around him. "But she died anyway, and you weren't there."

He flinched, tried not to reel from the blow she had dealt. "I would have been," he said, "if I'd known where she was." He swallowed hard. "All I ever wanted was to keep her safe."

Jann bit her lip, as though uncertain what to say next. He tried not to care what she thought, not to say more just to convince her. It couldn't matter what she thought if he was going to get Claire's son.

"Claire didn't want you to come," Jann said at last, "because she didn't want you to find out about Alex."

"What?" Peter said, stunned by Jann's words.

"She said you wouldn't understand."

"Understand what?" That his sister had had a baby and needed all the help he could give her. All the love.

"That Alex wasn't some project needing funding you'd refused to provide in the past."

"I told you why I couldn't support her in the life that she was choosing!"

"Alex was her flesh and blood," Jann doggedly went on. "He was everything she had."

"And now you have him." Something he couldn't allow to continue. She seemed to care for his sister's baby, but was a woman much like his mother. She lived an alternative lifestyle that would eventually leave no room for a child, no matter how much she declared she loved him.

"You saw your chance," he went on, "to get what Claire

had." He pressed his lips together. "What did you say to convince her to give you her baby and her money?"

The minute he said the words, he wished he hadn't spoken. If he'd blown her up with air and stuck her with a pin, the effect would have been the same. She seemed to fight for breath as though the air around her had vanished.

"Claire did what she felt she had to do," she finally gasped out. "What you pushed her to do! I didn't even know she wanted me to have custody of Alex until the lawyer had been to the hospital and drawn up the papers. Claire begged me to agree." Jann jutted her chin forward. "She asked me to promise. And I did."

"Promises can be broken." Like his mother's promises had been. His father's, too, only in a different way, with a different kind of hurt.

"Claire knew I always keep my promises." Jann passed her tongue over her lips. "And I intend to keep this one."

# Chapter Six

Jann groaned as the towering pile of freshly folded baby clothes tipped and re-joined the mound on the floor. She picked up a tiny undershirt and smoothed it over her knee. Usually, she enjoyed folding Alex's things, found it soothing to inhale the delicate aroma of baby soap clinging to his clothes, but after everything she and Peter had said to each other the night before, she was in no mood to be soothed.

Perhaps he would be late this morning.

Perhaps he wouldn't come back at all. Jann sighed. There was little chance of that.

She dreaded seeing him as much as she dreaded the effect he had on her. How could she engage in this struggle for custody of Alex when every time Peter came near, her pulse revved up like a racing car spinning around a track?

"Here's the little lamb," Ruby cooed, emerging from the narrow passageway leading to Alex's cabin with the baby settled on her hip. "All changed and ready for action."

"I'll take him," Jann said, with a grateful smile at Ruby. She nudged the collapsed pile of clothes away with her foot and held out her arms.

"His cheeks are awfully red," she said, settling Alex onto her lap. She glanced swiftly at Ruby. "Do you think he has a fever?"

Her friend placed the palm of her hand on Alex's forehead. "Cool," she pronounced.

"Thank goodness you're a nurse," Jann said, sighing with relief. "I don't know what I'd do without you and John."

"You'd do just fine," Ruby said, chuckling. "It's us who would be miserable without you and this wee fellow. I knew when I retired I would miss my work, but meeting the two of you has helped more than you know." She gave Jann's shoulder a warm squeeze.

"That's not to say, though," Ruby added, "that I think you're right, bringing up this little one the way you are."

"What do you mean?"

"You don't get out enough, honey. You spend all your time working or taking care of Alex. It isn't healthy." Ruby's eyes looked worried. "Not for you or the baby."

"It's what I like best," Jann said softly, gently stroking Alex's cheek. He flung out one chubby fist in an attempt to capture her hand. "Besides, what you said isn't true. I see you and John, and . . . and . . ." Fruitlessly, she searched for the names of other friends she'd seen lately. "Mitch!" she exclaimed finally, casting a triumphant look in Ruby's direction.

"Mitch!" Ruby snorted. "You haven't seen him socially in a dog's age."

"Well if that's so, now's not the time to start. I'm not going anywhere until Peter Strickland goes back where he belongs."

"Now there's a man to consider." A sly gleam appeared in Ruby's eyes. "Tall, handsome, and smart, too. You could do worse."

"He doesn't like me," Jann said flatly, "and I don't like him." Heat scorched her cheeks. She buried her face in Alex's chest so Ruby wouldn't see the damning color.

"You don't know him well enough to dislike him," Ruby protested.

"Claire knew him well enough and you know how she felt."

"Maybe Claire was wrong. When a person's young . . ."

"He wanted to control her."

"He seems the sort of man who'd just want his sister to be safe."

"He has you fooled!"

"Have you asked him about it?"

"Last night." Jann shuddered. "It's a long story."

"One that's got you rattled." Ruby looked at her shrewdly. "Maybe what he had to say made more sense than you want to admit."

"No! I—"

"Maybe Jann didn't like what she heard."

The sound of Peter's voice seemed to come out of nowhere, as did the sharp lurch to her heart. Glancing toward the companionway, Jann saw he was already halfway down the stairs.

Ruby was right, she decided, standing, her arms tightening protectively around her baby. Peter's story had thrown her, and she couldn't afford to be thrown if she meant to keep Alex.

"Sometimes the truth is hard to take," Peter added.

"I'll be on my way now, dear," Ruby said hastily, bustling past Jann and moving toward the stairs. "Nice to see you, Peter. Drop by our boat on your way out. Capt'n's got some pictures he wants to show you."

Escaping, that's what her friend was doing. Who could blame her? Jann waited until Ruby had slipped past Peter and disappeared up the companionway before fixing her gaze on Claire's brother.

"You want the truth?" she demanded softly, determined to finish now what she'd left unsaid the night before.

His gaze didn't falter.

"Claire thought if she told you about Alex, you would have taken him from her, too."

Some emotion flickered in Peter's eyes, but before she had a chance to assess it, he swept his hair from his forehead, his hand blocking her view.

"She knew me better than that," he said.

His words triggered a silence so deep it was impossible for Jann to continue. Did he expect her to believe him? To trust him? The only thing she knew for certain was that Claire's brother wanted Alex and was prepared to go to any lengths to get him.

She clutched her baby more tightly. Alex wiggled and twisted, his plump body suddenly an impossible weight in her arms. Nicely matching the leaden feeling in the pit of her stomach.

"Here," Peter said, holding out his arms, "give him to me."

Alex leaned toward his uncle's outstretched arms, squirming with anticipation.

"It's time for his nap," Jann lied, struggling to retain her grip. She turned, and swiftly made her way down the passage to the baby's cabin. Alex whimpered as she laid him in his crib.

"Shhh," she whispered, gently stroking his cheek, but his eyes screwed tighter and he began to cry. Slipping her crystal heart from around her neck, Jann dangled it in front of him. Alex loved the shiny stone, was usually soothed by it as much as she.

"Hush," she begged softly, praying Peter would go away.

The crystal worked its usual magic. Alex reached for it once or twice, then his eyes fluttered shut, flickered open once, then shut again. Jann tiptoed out of the cabin and slowly moved back along the passage. Peter was still standing where she had left him and from the stubborn look on his face, he wasn't going anywhere.

An angry wail, filtered only by Alex's door, suddenly filled the cabin with sound.

"Doesn't sound tired to me," Peter remarked mildly.

"What would you know about it?" Jann muttered, wincing as the wailing continued.

"Enough to know that baby is not going to sleep." He brushed past her. "I'll get him."

"You will not," Jann said fiercely, chasing after Peter and grabbing his arm.

He turned to face her, the narrow passage impossibly tight for two people. One look at his lips and Jann's heart sank. Perhaps Ruby was right. Perhaps it was time to let a man into her life. Maybe then her knees wouldn't turn to rubber every time she came close to Claire's brother.

She yanked her hand from Peter's arm, but the rubbery knees didn't disappear. She was fooling herself if she thought another man might help.

Peter gave her a long, hard look, then continued on his way. He spoke soothingly to Alex before picking him up, continuing to murmur endearments when he held the baby in his arms.

Alex's sobs dulled to a whimper and his stiff straight body gradually melted against his uncle's contour.

Fierce, unexpected tears welled up in Jann's eyes. She spun around, fleeing back to the main cabin. She had come to believe if she tried hard enough she could escape the fate she knew was hers. But against her better judgment, she had let first Claire and then Alex into her life, convincing herself she would be safe, that they would be safe.

She had been wrong.

Claire had died.

Peter might win.

Fear, as black as a moonless night, settled around Jann, blocking the sunlight pouring in through the portholes and filling her heart with dread. She clutched her crystal heart, desperate to find strength.

"You're out of diapers," Peter said, appearing at the head of the passageway.

She gaped at him, stupefied, his comment so ordinary in other circumstances, even homey. But only in someone else's life, where a man, woman and baby were a family. Not here. Not now.

"How do you know?" she asked, grasping for something to say and finding only that.

"Alexander needed changing," he replied, with a shrug. "So I did it, then put him back to bed."

Claire's brother wasn't supposed to know how to change a baby. He wasn't supposed to be good at any of this.

"Could you go to the shop then, and get some more diapers?" Jann asked. That would get him gone.

"You do it," he said. "I'll stay with Alexander."

"Not without me, you won't."

"You're being ridiculous." He shook his head. "I'm hardly going to spirit Alexander away in the time it takes you to go to the store."

He was capable of anything.

"I'll get Ruby," she said, and moved toward the stairs.

Jann glanced up at the sun. Must be close to noon already. It had taken her nearly half an hour to go to the store and back but Alex must be asleep now. She couldn't hear a sound from HEART'S DESIRE as she hurried down the dock.

She stepped on board and paused, listening, by the open hatch. Not a sound, not of Peter, or Ruby, or Alex himself. With any luck Peter had left, and she'd find Ruby curled up on the settee reading. With a lighter heart, she stepped down the companionway, then halted abruptly on the bottom step.

A dozen piles of neatly folded baby clothes lay in front of her on the floor. Ruby must have worked like a Trojan to get all that done in the short time she'd been gone.

Thank you, Jann whispered silently.

"That didn't take long," Peter drawled, abruptly stepping out from the galley.

"You're still here," Jann said, stunned, stumbling down the last step. "Why?"

"Just putting away the dish towels." He held up empty hands. "I'm not making off with the silver," he added, with a chuckle.

"But where's Ruby?"

"She went home."

"And left you here alone?" Her voice rose, emerging close to a scream.

"I'm a big boy, Jann." He grinned at her, looking nothing like a boy, looking only like what he was, a very strong, very sexy, man. "I'm not afraid to stay alone."

"You know very well what I mean." Then her breath abandoned her chest. "Everything's all right, isn't it? Nothing's happened to the Capt'n?"

The teasing light left Peter's eyes and he stepped toward her, until he was so close, she gave up all attempt to re-capture her breath.

"It's all right, Jann," he reassured her. "Nobody's hurt." He frowned. "You're awfully quick to assume the worst."

Relief rushed through her like a flash flood down a creek bed. "It's usually better to expect the worst than be ambushed by it," she muttered.

"What's made you so wary?"

"People like you . . ." She twisted away, not wanting to seek refuge in his eyes. ". . . who turn up and expect to get everything they want, even if it's something that belongs to someone else."

"I don't believe that's the reason." He took hold of her shoulder and pulled her gently around. "Tell me," he demanded again. "Tell me what's hurt you so badly."

"That's none of your business."

"Everything about you is my business."

"Why? So you can hold it against me in court?"

His eyes flashed dangerously and his grip tightened. A current crackled between them as he pulled her to him. At least it appeared he was pulling her closer. He seemed also to be pushing her away. She felt in limbo. Not closer, not farther, but locked in his arms nonetheless.

Her lips parted, the tug of war she saw waging in his eyes being also played out in her heart. Desire stabbed her loins, and she pressed her eyes shut, praying for the strength to resist this man, wishing someone, anyone, was there to help.

But there was no one there. She was on her own.

As she had been for a long time.

Peter groaned, as if the final giving in to desire had ruptured the bond between mind and body and the rending had caused him pain. His lips met hers as a moving train meets the air. Exacting, unswerving, relentless, his tongue probed deep, exploring her mouth.

No matter what her brain demanded, her limbs turned to jelly and her blood to fire. She could no more thrust Peter aside than stop the passage of time. And she admitted reluctantly . . . exultantly, she didn't want to.

His hands spread possessively along her back, caressing and kneading her skin until her nerve endings were ablaze. She flowed toward him like water into a chasm, her warmth seeking his as a moth seeks a flame. Her brain shrieked for release before she became consumed, but even if her body had obeyed, his did not. His hands were like steel draped in silk— soft enough to drive her desires to desperation—strong enough to hold her for all eternity.

He explored her lips unhindered, trailing kisses across her cheek to her neck. Then she arched backward, helpless with need as his mouth paved a path down her throat to her breasts. Her breathing all but ceased.

Far away, in the distant recesses of conscious thought, she felt the niggling pull of fear. If her passions raged out of control, she would lose everything.

Not only her soul, but Alex as well.

But beyond that lay a deeper fear, that the desire she felt was false, that it would die as it had always done in the past, leaving her cold and untouched.

She moaned, her lips dry with longing, and her chest heaved, air rushing into where, only an instant before, there had been none. Summoning her last remaining shred of will, she placed her hands on Peter's chest and pushed.

His lips froze. "Damn," he swore softly, withdrawing as swiftly as he had pulled her to him.

For a long moment, he stared down at her, his face drawn and grim. He, too, seemed to be fighting for control. The breath expelled from his lungs came out in a downward blast of air—like the heat of a dragon about to devour its victim.

Swallowing hard, Jann stepped backward. Away from his reach, she struggled to ease the tightness in her throat and the pulsing need in her loins.

"We keep doing this," Peter said hoarsely.

"It has to stop."

"Yes," he agreed.

His single word sounded so final, Jann's racing heart stilled.

"I don't want it," she whispered, searching for the strength to believe her own words.

He simply stared at her.

"I don't need it. Especially not from you."

"You do need it," he said quietly. "That, and much more. But you're right about one thing." His jaw tightened. "It can't be from me." He turned to move away.

Some impulse urged her to hold out her hand to stop him, but she cradled her body instead, locking one hand under each arm.

"Why did Ruby leave?" she asked, desperate to talk of other things, not wanting to think now of how he affected her.

"I told her there was no need to stay." He shrugged, the movement strangely stilted, as though his muscles no longer did his bidding.

"You told her to go?"

"Yes."

"That's my decision, not yours."

"Is it?" He went to the settee and scooped up two piles of

the baby clothes. They looked ridiculously small in his large hands.

"You know it is!"

"Not for much longer."

Jann's head began to spin as she tried to focus. Impossible, while looking into Peter's eyes. She stared at his hands instead.

"What are you doing with Alex's things?"

"Thought I'd put them away. I like to finish what I start."

"Didn't Ruby fold those clothes?"

"No." He smiled faintly. "I take it there's no difference in our technique?"

She angrily sucked in a breath. Access was one thing, but this man was beginning to dominate her life. And most irritating was the fact that she couldn't help but be impressed with the way he handled Alex. Besides playing with the baby, Peter changed diapers and folded laundry. Did things only a parent would want to do.

Without warning, he swept past her, carrying the clothes to Alex's cabin. Then within seconds, he was back for another load.

"Stop it!" she exclaimed, putting her hand on his arm. "I'll finish after you've gone."

"I'm not going anywhere," he said firmly, shaking off her hand and reaching for a stack of sleepers.

Then he looked at her, and his eyes darkened to a deeper green. He took one hesitant step toward her, as though not trusting himself to be close.

"I don't want to hurt you, Jann," he said softly. "That's never been what I wanted."

"If you try to take Alex, that's exactly what you will be doing."

"He'll be better off with me."

"He's best where he is."

"I think we should have dinner together."

"Together?" she repeated stupidly.

Two tiny undershirts spilled from the pile in Peter's hand and landed on the floor. "Yes," he said, ignoring the fallen clothes.

It was as though each drop of blood was magnified in Jann's veins, as though her hearing had become so acute she could identify the whirring of a dragonfly on deck.

"Yes," Peter said again, moving at last to snatch up the undershirts and tuck them under his arm.

Jann's mind swirled, and hysteria boiled through her, threatening to erupt. "Why?" she asked, again, fighting it back.

"So we can get to know each other."

"I don't want to know you." Even as she said them, Jann knew her words were false.

"It'll be easier for you if we get to know each other."

"Easier for me?" Jann demanded. "In what way would it be easier?" If Peter got custody of Alex, he would be the one feeding him, comforting him, watching her baby grow. The thought of that was not easy. She shook her head no.

"It will be easier," Peter said firmly. "Trust me."

# Chapter Seven

Trust him? Peter had asked the impossible.

Jann tried to relax against the green velvet covers of the plush upholstered chair, but she couldn't. Stupid kind of fabric for Hawaii. Too hot, too clingy. A cold weather sort of fabric—a Boston sort of fabric. Perhaps that's why Peter had chosen this particular restaurant. It was supposed to be one of the best, but she had never liked it, had never felt comfortable with its air of old money and old manners.

And it was not the sort of place for a confrontation. Perhaps that was why Peter had chosen it.

"He's late," Jann said, for the second time, peering into the topaz eye of the silver dragon writhing around her wrist. In the restaurant's subdued lighting, she could barely make out the numbers on the eye's spherical surface.

"We're early," Mitch replied mildly, glancing at his own watch.

She leaned forward, thumping her elbows on to the table. "We'll give him five more minutes, then I'm leaving."

"Oh no you're not," Mitch protested. "I've been asking you out to dinner for months and we're finally doing it."

"This isn't a date, Mitch."

"Maybe not, but it's the closest I've had so far. I'm not leaving until we've ordered, eaten, and chatted over coffee."

She twisted around and shot another glance toward the entrance.

"Stop fidgeting," Mitch said sternly. "There's no reason to be nervous."

"There's every reason."

"Things have been going well, haven't they?"

"If you call putting up with a stranger hanging around every minute of the day well."

"Has he behaved badly in any way?"

Only kissed her so thoroughly she now dreamed about it all the time. Even when awake, she imagined she felt his lips on hers. Yes, he'd been behaving badly, but so had she, and try as she might, she couldn't blame it all on him.

"Has he been good with Alex?"

Jann sighed, the knot in the pit of her stomach now the size of a pineapple. "Yes," she admitted glumly, "he's been good."

"Then what's the problem?"

"I just don't want to see him any more often than is necessary. And he's made friends with John and Ruby."

Mitch placed his hand over hers and for a moment she felt comforted. Until she remembered another hand and the emotions it had evoked. She sighed again.

"Making friends does not mean he's going to win custody," Mitch said soothingly.

"It can't hurt," Jann replied, misery eating at her gut. "I don't trust him."

"Trust who?"

At the sound of Peter's voice, she started and spun around. "Peter," she breathed, then in the next breath, "You're late."

"Right on time," he said equably, without glancing at his watch. He did look at Mitch, and though Peter neither spoke nor moved, Jann felt compelled to explain.

"This is Mitch Zachery," she said, unsure how Peter would react. She had asked Mitch along thinking safety in numbers, but it wasn't Peter who's behavior she feared the most. It was her own lack of control, when she was near him, or touched him, or . . . .

She couldn't go on thinking of how good his lips had felt, or try to imagine what it would be like to feel his bare skin against her body. She didn't want to get closer to this man who was her enemy, who wanted only one thing from her and that was her son.

Peter nodded at Mitch, then looked back at her. Explain, his expression ordered, without him uttering a word.

"Mitch is a friend of mine," she said slowly. "I hope you don't mind my inviting him along." The room seemed to have tightened, becoming almost claustrophobic.

"If this is awkward . . ." Mitch pushed back his chair and stood.

Peter was taller than her friend and though leaner, was more powerful. Like a tightly coiled spring next to a comfy stuffed bear.

"Don't go, Mitch," Jann said swiftly, begging him with a look. She didn't want to be alone with Peter, not after that kiss, not here where it seemed like a date.

"By all means, join us," Peter offered, politely holding out his hand. After Mitch shook it, Peter sat down opposite Jann, his green eyes gazing directly into hers.

As they had when he had kissed her.

Her face flushed with heat. She wanted to clutch her crystal heart and wish herself away. If only her necklace had that power.

"I've not seen you around Jann's boat," Peter commented to Mitch.

"Mitch is my lawyer," Jann explained, meeting Peter's sharp glance with her chin held high.

"This was supposed to be a friendly meeting," Peter said, with a frown.

"Mitch is here as my friend."

Peter lifted one brow, his gaze again probing hers, as though he knew what she was thinking and why she'd brought Mitch along.

"How's Alex tonight?" Mitch asked, changing the subject.

"Fine," Jann answered tersely, wishing the change hadn't been to that of Alex, not now in front of Peter. But perhaps that didn't matter. Whether spoken about or not, the baby was as present in everyone's minds as if he were there in the flesh, for it was he who connected them one to the other, made them adversaries when all she'd ever wanted was peace.

"What do you think of the little guy?" Mitch continued on.

Inwardly, Jann groaned.

"He looks just like Claire," Peter replied, his expression warming.

"More like you," Jann said softly.

"Does he?" Peter asked, his brows lifting in surprise.

"Yes," she whispered, unable to regret the pleasure she saw in his eyes.

"Last time I looked he was a squalling ball of wrinkles and redness," Mitch said, with a grin, then ducked to avoid the flat-handed swipe Jann aimed at his shoulder.

"If you had come out of your office and seen him the last time we were there, you . . ." Jann swallowed hard. The last time she and Alex had been in Mitch's office was for the purpose of discussing Peter's access to her baby.

Peter seemed to notice her discomfort and held out his hand towards her. "Dance, Ms. Fletcher?"

"We've not ordered yet," Jann protested, afraid to touch him.

"There's no rush."

"Mitch—"

"Will be fine without us."

Mitch smiled amiably and nodded his agreement.

With reluctance, Jann took hold of Peter's hand and moved with him onto the dance floor. Other couples were already out there, swaying in each others' arms.

Without speaking, he drew her close, placing one hand on the small of her back, the other around her fingers, enclosing them, warming them.

It felt strange dancing with Peter, yet in another way oddly comfortable, as though they had done it a thousand times before. Perhaps too comfortable. Jann stiffened.

"Relax," Peter said.

"Impossible," she muttered.

"Why?"

"You know why."

"Because we kissed?"

"Yes," she said, avoiding his eyes. She stared at his chin, instead, noticing he had shaved before coming out for the evening, wondering how his skin would feel next to hers.

"Forget the kiss," he growled. "I have."

She looked into his eyes now, almost losing herself in their depths. "You're lying," she accused.

His shoulders tensed.

"Maybe I am," he finally admitted, "but it's probably best we pretend it never happened."

"Because I'm a gold-digging baby-snatcher?"

"Ouch," Peter said, wincing.

"Do you still think that?" If she could have pulled the question back, she would have. She couldn't allow herself to care what he thought. Not and hang on to Alex, too.

"I haven't figured you out yet," he said, looking at her thoughtfully. "I think you're warm, and funny—"

"No one's ever accused me of being funny before."

"Only when you're angry," he explained, his eyes now dancing, the tension between them dissolving. "You have a funny way of wrinkling your nose and . . ." He shrugged, not finishing what he was about to say. "I haven't figured out yet whether you have a sense of humor as a rule."

"Meaning what?" she asked.

"Mostly, I see you irritable and cross."

"With good reason," she replied.

"Yes," he agreed, "but you have to come to terms with the fact Alex will inevitably be coming with me. Have to learn to live with that."

"Never."

"May I cut in?" Mitch asked, coming up behind Peter and tapping on his shoulder.

Peter's gaze remained on hers, his arms around her waist as hard as his scrutiny.

"Yes," Jann agreed quickly, one part of her exulting in the displeasure crossing Peter's face as he realized that everything wasn't necessarily going his way.

"Did I interrupt something?" Mitch murmured, after she had withdrawn from Peter's arms.

She didn't answer, simply watched as Peter walked slowly back to their table.

"You looked as though you needed rescuing," Mitch added gently.

"Just dance with me," she whispered, wrapping her arms around his neck.

"Gladly," he agreed, pulling her close.

Her heart felt heavy and her body did too, as though her usual lightness of spirit was imprisoned within. Mitch's scent wasn't Peter's scent, and his warmth not Peter's either.

She'd been so relieved to be free of Peter's presence, and now, an instant later, was filled with regret. If only for the space of a dance, she wished she could expunge Claire's brother from her mind and soul.

A dance both too long and too short, Jann decided, when she and Mitch returned to the table. Peter was sitting there, alone. It caught her heart, his aloneness, and she became wrenchingly aware that he needed Alex as much as she.

But Alex needed a mother, she told herself determinedly, and no matter how much Peter tried, he couldn't take a mother's place.

"I'm going home now," Mitch said, pulling out Jann's chair for her, but not sitting down himself.

"Don't go," Jann protested, not wanting to sound desperate, but praying her friend would know she was.

"Glad to have met you," Peter said briskly, standing to shake Mitch's hand.

"You haven't eaten yet, Mitch" Jann said, glaring at Peter.

"I'm not hungry," her friend replied, "and you both look as though you've got things to say."

"Nothing I wouldn't want you hearing," Jann insisted.

"Should my lawyer be present as well?" Peter asked.

"I told you," Jann snapped, "Mitch isn't here as my lawyer."

Peter's eyebrows rose.

"He's here as my friend."

"And your friend is going home," Mitch said firmly. "I've got an early start in the morning."

He took hold of Jann's hand and held it for a moment between his palms. His touch soothed and comforted, then, dropping her hand, he threw her to the wolf.

"Call if you need me," he instructed, waving a genial goodbye.

"Nice fellow," Peter said.

"He can be very tough in court."

"Glad you warned me," Peter said, infuriating her with a smile.

"Don't underestimate him," Jann warned. "Or me either."

"Not a mistake I'd make again." His expression sobered. "Are you and that lawyer an item?"

"What do you mean?"

"Are you going together, dating?"

"No," Jann said slowly, suddenly wishing that they were. Maybe with the possibility of a real family, a real home, her position as Alex's mother would be strengthened.

"He's interested in you," Peter said, his eyes narrowing shrewdly.

She shrugged. She hadn't dated Mitch seriously for the

same reason she dated few men more than once. She couldn't risk that sort of bond in her life right now, couldn't risk the kind of pain it was sure to bring.

"So what's your type if it isn't Mitch?"

"I don't have a type."  Crossly, she noted that her heart was racing again, and that all it had taken was a look from Peter's eyes.

"Tall, short, blonde, dark?"

"My type is men who don't ask questions they have no business asking."

"Everything about you is my business."

"What do you mean?"

"For the moment you've got my baby. I want to know who you are."

"The same holds true for me."  She looked at him appraisingly. "Do you have a girlfriend?"  Her cheeks warmed. Surely if he did, he wouldn't have kissed her, wouldn't have made her toes tingle with the force of electricity between them.

"What makes you think I'm not married?"

Married. The beating of her heart seemed to stop with a thump. Impossible to imagine him forever joined to another woman, one, who if Peter won, would become the mother of her child.

What sort of woman would she be? Dark like Peter or blonde in striking contrast? Would she be petite and in need of protection, or tall and slimly elegant? And her voice, would it be like Peter's flawlessly enunciated Boston accent? Perfect in every way?

Jann swallowed hard, then felt relief as the realization hit her. "If you were married you would have said so. If you were married you wouldn't have kissed me."

"Plenty of married men kiss other women," he replied, in a voice so bitter it cut the air between them.

"Not you," she said, with a certainty that stunned.

"What makes you think so?"

She shook her head, unwilling to speak her thoughts out loud, that when this man married it would be a union that would last forever.

"What about a girlfriend?" she asked, wanting to turn the conversation away from talk of wedded bliss.

"Applying for the position?" he asked, a grin streaking his lips.

"Never!" The very notion rendered her dizzy. To be with a man like him, to be held in his powerful arms, though thrilling to contemplate, was terrifying in the extreme. "You haven't answered my question," she reminded him hastily.

"No girlfriend at the moment," he replied, with a shrug.

He looked the sort of man who was never alone for long, who had only to click his fingers to render the female of the species weak. Not the sort of man she could ever allow herself to fall in love with.

"Why this sudden interest in my love life?" he asked.

"Just trying to figure out who you are."

"Have you come to any conclusions?"

"Some."

"Tell me," he ordered, then wished that he hadn't asked her. It shouldn't matter what this woman thought. He couldn't let it matter.

"Claire told me you were away traveling a lot of the time," Jann replied, not answering his question at all.

"Off and on," he said. Two could play the evasive game. "What about you? Do you like to travel?"

"I would love to give it a try, but I've not been any place but here."

"Where would you like to go?" He tried not to notice the way her face lit up, with a glow independent of the flickering candle on their table.

"Anywhere," she breathed.

"Miami?" he asked. "The French Riviera?" That's where his mother had gone, before she'd become enmeshed in the counter culture sweeping America, before telling Peter's father that their marriage vows were old-fashioned and that she was a free spirit.

"No," Jann answered definitely. "I want to go somewhere more interesting, somewhere out of the way."

Her eyes were glowing now, also, in a way he'd never seen.

"Like South America or Africa," she continued dreamily. Then she looked at him curiously. "Have you been there?"

"Yes," he answered shortly, fighting to banish the sudden image of her striding through an African village, of being surrounded at a riverside by a splashing group of black-eyed children. "You'd love it," he said hoarsely.

"Like you do?"

"Yes," he answered honestly.

"If travel means so much to you, then why do you want Alex? How will a baby fit into your life?"

"I'll make him fit."

She laughed, a deep-throated explosion of amusement. "It's been my experience," she said, trying to form the words between hiccups of mirth, "that babies make you fit them, not the other way around." Then her expression sobered. "What's a bachelor like you going to do with a baby?"

"Don't worry about how I'll do it. Just trust that I will."

"I don't trust you," Jann said quietly, "any more than Claire did."

"Then you'll have to learn," he replied tightly, hurt spiraling through him at the mention of his sister, how she'd never know now just how much he had loved her, and how their connection as children would never extend to adulthood.

"I don't have to learn anything," Jann replied stubbornly.

"I'd like to take Alexander out tomorrow," Peter said, changing the subject.

"That's not a good idea."

"What do you mean?"

"He's getting too used to you."

"He trusts me, you mean." Sharp pleasure went through him at the thought, was dulled only in the knowledge the woman opposite didn't feel it too.

"Used to you," she repeated, her lower lip trembling as though she feared his words were true. "I don't want him getting used to someone who will soon disappear."

"I wouldn't worry about that."

For a long moment she looked at him, then with a sigh said, "I guess he can go. But not without me."

"I wouldn't dream of taking him without you," Peter replied, feeling strangely lighthearted. Was it due to the notion of sharing the day with Claire's child, or the fact that Jann would be there as well? It had to be the first, for the second was impossible.

"Where will we go?" she asked.

"I was thinking perhaps a picnic."

"A picnic!"

"You know, cold chicken, chocolate cake, a bottle of wine."

"I know what a picnic is."

"Then say yes. It'll be fun."

"Fun?"

The expression on her face told him he was suggesting the unattainable, that nothing had been fun since he'd put in his claim for Alex. Perhaps she didn't feel what he felt whenever they were together, and if that were the case, then he should feel relieved.

For these feelings he was beginning to harbor for her would have to be pushed aside. He couldn't risk caring for a woman like Jann, a woman who lived on a boat and took pictures for a living. She might claim she loved Alex now, but what about in six months time when the child was bigger, more demanding?

When he got in the way of her independent life?

As he and Claire had got in the way of their mother's new life. The muscles along Peter's jaw line tightened. He had to take Claire's baby. Anything else was unthinkable.

"When will we go?" Jann asked reluctantly.

"I'll pick you both up at ten."

"I'm busy in the morning. Better make it the afternoon."

She was wearing her stubborn look again.

"And I don't need anyone to pick me up," she went on firmly. "Alex and I will come for you."

"You have no car," he objected.

"I have access to one when I need it," she replied airily. "We'll pick you up at noon."

# Chapter Eight

"Please, Capt'n," Jann wheedled. "You know you promised I could borrow your van if I ever needed it."

Capt'n's gray brows beetled fiercely at her. "That was before you stripped out second gear, girl."

"John Miller!" Ruby exclaimed. "Just listen to yourself. Blaming Jann for that gear." She snorted disgustedly. "You know very well you stripped it yourself. You were so busy cursing out the driver in front of you, you paid no attention to your own business." She turned to Jann. "His teeth were grinding together so fiercely it was impossible to tell which noise was louder, the one coming from his mouth or the one from the transmission!"

Jann stifled a giggle by planting a kiss onto Alex's hair.

"Damn it, Ruby," Capt'n protested, "I thought we agreed to forget about that."

"Lend Jann the car and we might," Ruby said, placing her hands on her hips and staring at him sternly.

"Harumph," Capt'n said. He turned his back on her and slapped a streak of brown stain across *WINDWARD*'s wooden deck. "The keys are hanging inside the door," he added gruffly.

"Thanks, Capt'n," Jann said, plopping a swift peck also on his weathered cheek.

"Now, girl . . ." He rubbed his cheek, trying, without success, to erase the smile lifting his lips. "Just be careful with it," he blustered.

"Aye, aye, Capt'n," Jann said, shifting Alex to her other arm and saluting smartly. She took the keys from Ruby's outstretched hand and pressed a kiss onto her cheek. "Thanks, Ruby," she whispered.

The doorman was too well trained to even blink when the

Capt'n's van sputtered up between the marble pillars of the hotel entrance. But before the doorman could reach the door, Peter had wrenched it open.

"You have got to be joking," he said.

"Joking?" Jann opened her eyes wide. "About what?"

"This death trap you call a vehicle."

"This is a vintage Volkswagen," she explained, lovingly stroking the vehicle's steering wheel. "It was at Woodstock."

"Attending a rock concert thirty or more years in the past does not speak well for reliability," Peter contested grimly.

"Volkswagens are like wine," Jann countered. "They improve with age."

"Or turn to vinegar and this bucket of bolts appears to be doing the latter. I won't allow my nephew to ride in a car that's about to break down."

"So how did you get around in New Guinea," she asked. "From the documentaries I've seen on television the mode of transport there appeared to be pick-up trucks." She leaned toward him and smiled. "With the most people possible jammed in the back."

"That was then. This is now."

But she could see his lips were twitching. Stifling her own grin, she twisted the knob on the glove compartment, and reached inside.

"Would this help you feel more comfortable?" she asked, pulling out a gold medal and dangling it in front of his face.

Slowly, Peter reached for it. "First," he read aloud, "in the First Annual Cross Oahu Race." Disbelief flickered across his face. "You expect me to be impressed by speed?"

"Isn't that the standard most men go by?"

"Not this man," Peter muttered, peering into the back where Alex cooed peacefully at him from behind the plastic steering wheel attached to his car seat.

"John worked for an entire year on this car," Jann went on

indignantly. "The engine runs like a dream. Not a sputter, not a knock, nothing that shouldn't be there is there. He's an engineer for God's sake."

"That doesn't mean he's a mechanic!"

"More a mechanic than you or I!"

Peter glared at her, then the earlier twitching of his lips turned into a laugh. "All right," he capitulated, climbing into the front beside her, "we'll risk your chariot."

The food, at least, looked wonderful, Jann decided, glad she had insisted on providing the picnic. Peter had paid for the dinner the night before, squelching her protest that they split the cost. At least now she would no longer be beholden to this man who could control her fate.

She pulled out some ripe bananas from the bottom of her shopping bag and laid them on a spot not already taken up. She'd bought too much, she decided with a sigh. A common occurrence whenever she went to the market.

The fresh fruit and vegetables always called to her like sirens called sailors, and proved irresistible in their glistening coats. She'd bought a pineapple as well as the bananas, and mangoes, too, from old Sarah's fruit stand, and still-warm baguettes from Francoise's stall.

The French woman had looked at her curiously when Jann purchased a triangle of the stall's best brie and thin slivers of Canadian smoked salmon. She'd even asked what the occasion was. But Jann had simply smiled and said she, Alex and a friend were taking a picnic to the Polynesian Cultural Center.

It might be too much, but it was a picnic fit for a king, Jann decided, well contented with the spread. Even a rich man from Boston would find no cause for complaint. Although to be fair, after the initial protest against Jann's van, Peter had been a good sport. When the Volkswagen stalled at a stop light, he'd merely looked at her with an I-told-you-so grin and slipped out quietly to check under the hood.

"Needs a tune-up, maybe," Jann had muttered as they'd peered into the engine together, and later, after Peter had fiddled with this belt and that clamp, she had held her breath as she turned the key in the ignition. His tinkering worked. Without a single hesitation the engine turned over and idled smoothly.

She had exaggerated a little about the vehicle's capabilities. She hadn't told Peter there had been only three entries in the race, or that it had begun as a joke between old friends. Two other retirees had bought claptrap old wrecks about the same time as John and they'd laughingly challenged each other to a race.

One year later, when the cars were fixed up, the Cross Oahu race was born. To the amazement of all, John had come in first, a fact of which he was inordinately proud, and about which Ruby teased him unmercifully.

Jann glanced at Peter watching a Cultural Center performer crack open a coconut on the tip of a stake. Only he wasn't looking at the demonstration. He was concentrating instead on the baby in his arms.

"Lunch is ready," she called, restraining her impulse to dash forward and snatch her baby away. Claire's brother was becoming so comfortable with Alex, and Alex was comfortable too. Like the perfect father and son. A family. Jann's pulse thudded against her temple. A family without her.

"Everything looks wonderful," Peter said, turning at her call and approaching the picnic table. He reached out his hand and snagged a skewer of pineapple from the fruit platter.

"You sound surprised," Jann said.

"Not at all."

Something in his tone warmed her, and the warmth was frightening, too, making her long to run towards him and at the same time run away. "I need Alex's car seat," she said breathlessly. "I'll just go get it."

"What do we need it for?"

"Alex can sit in it while we eat."

"I'll hold him."

"No," she said swiftly, perhaps too swiftly, for his brows lifted inquiringly.

"I'll go," he offered.

"No," she said again, managing with effort to keep her voice level. She turned and moved in the direction of the car park, needing to be away from him for a few moments to keep her thoughts at bay.

He caught up to her and placed his hand on her arm, slowing her, stopping her. Her turmoil increased.

"We'll all go," he said firmly.

She nodded reluctantly, and together they walked out through the Cultural Center's gates.

"So," he began, casting her a smile as they wove between the parked cars, "are you having fun yet?"

"How can I have fun?" she demanded wearily, too aware of him as usual and overwhelmed by his presence.

"Why can't you?"

"Because nothing has changed. No matter how normally we try to behave, how many dinners we have out, picnics we conjure up, or trips to the zoo, we're still in the same place." The pulse hammering her temples increased to a pounding. "We both still want the same thing but both of us can't have what we want."

"That's true," he admitted slowly, "but I was hoping you were beginning to see that Alex will be happy with me."

She didn't want to even look at Alex, couldn't bear to see more evidence that what Peter said was true, couldn't bear, either, the thought of Alex leaving. When had she become so attached to this child? The first moment she saw him, she realized with despair.

"In other words," she said starkly, "you win and I lose."

"I wouldn't put it like that."

"There's no other way to put it." She turned away, desperate to hide the moisture gathering in her eyes, not wanting to look weak when she needed to be strong. Swiftly, she moved the last few steps to the van.

"Wait!" Peter cried, catching up with her as she jerked open the door. Juggling Alex in his arms, he pulled her around so that all she could see now was his face. "It's time to face facts," Peter said brusquely, but the eyes staring into hers were gentle.

"What facts?"

"It's time to give Alexander up."

"Why?" she demanded, resisting the urge to snatch her baby from him. "So you can catch the plane tomorrow and take Alex with you? No more time wasted. Everything tidy and as it should be." She glared at him over Alex's head. "That's not going to happen."

"I was wanting this to be easier for you."

"You just want it easier for yourself."

"I don't want to hurt you."

"Then leave my baby be."

"I can't," he said. "Surely you can see that."

She could see it and that's what made it all so difficult. If Claire's brother loved his nephew even half as much as she, he would never give up his quest.

"I'll have to stay here until you change your mind," he said, handing Alex to her, then reaching past her to lift Alex's car seat from the van. With his movement, he was close to her, could feel her breath upon his neck. He clenched his jaw, determined to resist the call her body made to his.

"Have you considered Alex in all of this?" She stepped away from him as she spoke, as if she, too, felt the call.

The loss of her nearness was both a sorrow and a relief. "Alex is the only one I am considering," he said gruffly. Now

that Claire was dead, he couldn't allow himself to think of anyone else, couldn't continue to be attracted to this woman who
had been Claire's friend.

"A baby needs a mother."

Her voice was so low, it almost disappeared, as the life died
in her eyes when he spoke of taking Alex. He tried to harden
his heart, tried not to care. For Alexander's sake. For his own.

"Mothers aren't always what they appear," he said tightly.

"What do you mean?"  She drew herself up, her hair
around her head now a bristling halo of indignation.

It seemed suddenly as if there were a wall between himself
and her, that if he reached for her the wall would be palpable
to the touch. Was it an aura he was seeing? Was he starting to
think like she thought now? If he stayed in her company
much longer, would he, too, believe in crystals and the power
of the spirit.

As his mother had believed. Or so she had said.

Old age hippie, new age free spirit. Not a speck of difference between them as far as he could see. Though in his opinion, his mother had come too late to the movement, wasn't
really interested in the hope and innocence of that era, wanted nothing to do with the peace and justice issues, wanted
only the freedom to indulge in her own desires.

"Alex needs someone he can depend on," he said fiercely,
forcing his arms to his sides, not allowing them to move lest
he take them both in his grasp.

"He can depend on me."

The magic was back in her eyes once more. He had to fight
its pull, couldn't let himself surrender, for if he put himself at
risk, Alexander would be at risk, also, and he couldn't let that
happen again to someone he loved.

"Can you promise you'll be around for the next twenty
years?" he demanded.

Pain streaked her face and lodged in her eyes. "No one can

guarantee that," she whispered.

He wanted to hold her, comfort her, never let her go. "That's what's required," he said instead.

A lifetime commitment was something his mother had never understood. She had enjoyed her children only when it was convenient, but was too swiftly bored and eager to escape with people as rich and bored as herself, giving no thought at all to the family she left behind. She bestowed on others the attention he and Claire had needed, hadn't seen that without their mother, a child's heart could break.

It had happened to Claire. He wouldn't let it happen to Claire's child.

"I know what's required," Jann replied breathlessly, as though no air had made its way from her throat to her lungs, as though she continued to stand through sheer will power alone, "and what I intend, but—"

"There are no buts."

"No one knows what the future holds." Her face paled as though she'd already looked through the door to the future, and never again wanted to look that way.

"Take control of the present and the future will take care of itself," Peter advised firmly.

"You can't control the present or the future either. No one can."

"Then how can you take charge of a baby?" He saw the hurt in her eyes, longed to somehow eradicate it. "No one will blame you, Jann, if you give up Alex now. You're young. You're not tied down. He's not your blood."

"I love him," she said simply.

His mother had said the same, when speaking of him and Claire, but he'd discovered that without care, the words meant nothing.

"Love's not enough," he growled. "You can't say you want him now, then lose interest when something more interesting comes along."

"There's nothing more interesting to me than Alex."

The way she looked at his sister's baby, he could almost believe she meant it.

"I've seen how you live," he countered, "and your passion for your work. What happens when you can't do both?"

"Alex is my passion."

"Maybe today. But what about next week, next month, next year?"

"I made a promise."

"What happens when you wake up one morning and realize just how tied down you are?"

Jann swallowed hard, his words jolting her, turning her cold. She'd spent half a lifetime keeping herself free, warding off emotional commitments like a fish would a shark. And now with this baby, she was prepared to fling her freedom away and would welcome the tie to another human being.

"I don't look upon custody of Alex as tying myself down," she said, aware of a lightening in the area of her heart. It was true what she said, and the knowledge gave her joy.

"What about a husband?"

"I don't need a husband."

"You say that now, but what will you say when you meet someone you like?"

"I'm not intending to fall in love." Heat warmed her cheeks as she made her denial and she lowered her gaze, not sure what was in her eyes. Or in her heart either. She only knew that in some strange way Peter Strickland was starting to get to her, to mean more to her than was wise. She was equally sure she couldn't afford for him to know.

"People never intend to fall in love," Peter told her solemnly.

"I thought you didn't believe in love."

"I don't."

"It could happen just the same."

"It won't."

"And if you do fall in love, what then? If you have Alex he'll be in your way, too."

"Babies are seldom convenient," he asserted, flinging back at her what she'd said to him. "Mostly they just happen, like Alexander happened for Claire."  He bent and kissed Alex's head, their dark hair mingling. "You don't turn your back and say, not now, thank you very much."

"I didn't turn my back," Jann cried. "Alex has me to take care of him. You're not obligated to react to anything. Claire wanted me to have Alex and I want him, too. He's safe. He's loved."

"He's my nephew," Peter said, "and I don't want to talk about this anymore."

"Afraid?" she demanded.

"No," he replied coldly.

"Every time we speak of love and marriage in relation to you, you try to change the subject."

"Your questions are too personal."

"No more personal than what you asked me."  She stared at him hard. "I'd like to know the answer. Besides, you seem to know a lot about me, so no doubt you've had your lawyers working overtime on that. I'm entitled to ask questions too."

"You're entitled to nothing."

"You're afraid," she accused again then ruthlessly went on. "The woman you fall in love with might not care that Alex is your nephew. She'd probably prefer to have her own children than care for someone else's."

"The same could be said about you."  His words smashed against her like storm waters against the shore.

"I don't want my own children," she denied, feeling her lips tremble, knowing as she spoke that what she said was a lie. "Alex is all I want. All I need. To me," she finished starkly,

"Alex is everything."

Jann wearily put the last of the picnic dishes into the galley cupboards, wishing the words she and Peter had spoken would stop reverberating in her brain.

They had taken a stab at eating the feast she had brought, but neither had been very hungry. When at last they finished trying, Peter had packed up the food and dishes, while she wandered the Cultural Center with Alex in the stroller.

She had managed somehow then to control her brain's whirling, but it was impossible to do so now in the silence of her own space.

"Are you alone?" Peter asked, his voice coming from somewhere behind her.

"What are you doing here?" she cried, whirling to face him again. She should no longer be startled by Peter's sudden appearances, should be used to his frequent comings and goings. But the truth was, each time she saw him, the electricity between them grew, reaching for her like a magnetic current and jolting her into connection.

He swept one broad palm through his thick hair, pushing it back and away from his face. "I came to say goodnight to Alexander," he explained.

Jann touched the crystal around her neck and was grateful for its coolness. She needed it tonight to protect herself from this man.

"I wasn't expecting you," she whispered, wishing her heart would stop its pounding, trying hard now to remember that this man was her enemy.

"I wanted time with Alexander."

"He's asleep."

"That's what you always say."

"That's what babies mostly do." She smiled faintly. "You've already spent a lot of time with him today."

"Which is a good thing. I want him to feel comfortable with me when you go away."

Her blood seemed to freeze as it coursed through her veins.

His eyebrows lifted. "I'm not mistaken, am I? You are going to Maui tomorrow?"

Jann swirled her tongue around the edges of her mouth, but was unable to find the moisture she needed.

"How did you find out?" she finally managed.

"Ruby," Peter said shortly.

"Ruby told you?" Jann's limbs grew heavy. If Peter could get around the best friend she had in the world, he'd have no trouble with a judge.

"She's worried about you going by yourself."

"Worried?"

"You better sit down. You look as though you're about to faint."

"I am not about to faint."

"Here's a chair."

"I don't need a chair. What I need is for you to go away and never come back."

"That's not going to happen." The steel in his voice shafted through to her heart. "I'm not leaving Hawaii without Alexander."

"You're not leaving with him."

"That'll be up to the courts."

"You're not to see him while I'm gone." She was too tired for this, hadn't the strength to fight this man.

"Who's going to stop me?"

"Ruby . . . and . . . and . . . John." Even as she spoke, Jann knew her friends would be useless. They could never hold out against a man like Peter Strickland, would not even try. For they had liked him enough to tell him her plans.

"I think it's time we re-think this supervised access thing," Peter said gently.

"What do you mean, re-think?" All heat seeped from her body, like water from a sieve.

"It's not working."

"It's working fine!"

"I intend to apply for unsupervised access."

Jann leaned against the cabin wall and spread her palms over the wood, seeking strength and support, but not finding either. Then her gaze fell on the photo of the aged Hawaiian woman, and the wisdom of centuries in the old woman's face. She would have found the strength to fight for her child. Jann clenched her fists. She could too.

"That won't be necessary," she said. "I'm sure when I get back we can come to some satisfactory solution."

"And while you're gone?"

She fought to control the trembling building in her heart. She bit her lip, the pain steadying her.

"Ruby was right," she said, ignoring his question.

"About what?" he asked.

How could she meet his eyes? He would read the truth in hers.

"I am sailing to Maui . . ." If she led into it slowly, perhaps the plan that had unexpectedly lodged in her brain wouldn't seem so impossible. "I plan to photograph the finish of the Victoria—Maui yacht race." She forced herself to look at him now. "I need someone to handle the boat while I take the pictures. Would you like to come along and do that?"

A long silence.

Jann waited, held her breath. If he accepted, it would be unbearable, even worse if he didn't.

"Let's see if I've got this right," Peter said slowly. "You don't want me to see Alexander while you're gone so you've concocted this plan to ensure that I don't."

She winced. He'd got it right.

"Plans like yours tend to backfire."

She was already regretting it.

"Call me crazy . . ." His lips widened into a grin. ". . .but I'd like to see what happens."

Her trembling ceased.

"I accept."

# Chapter Nine

Jann frowned. Alex's cheeks were awfully red. And his nose was running as if there were two feet of snow outside and he'd caught the granddaddy of all colds.

What if he were really sick? Chilled, she pushed the thought away. She would have him checked out first before allowing herself to worry, and if Alex was sick, she wouldn't be going to Maui. At least then she wouldn't have to spend three days alone with Peter Strickland.

Her only regret would be the race. Two years ago when the last one had been held, she had promised herself next time she would be at the finish line taking pictures. Two years ago, she hadn't had a buyer for her work. That had now changed. Her photos were becoming known.

None of which mattered. Not if Alex was sick. Gently, she rolled him onto his tummy and rubbed his back. He soon fell asleep, his body hot and restless beneath her hand.

"Ja . . . nn." Ruby's voice filtered towards her down the passage way.

"I'm in here with Alex," Jann softly called back. "I'll be right out." She tucked a cotton blanket around the baby and moved as quietly as she could back down the passage to the main cabin.

Capt'n was pacing restlessly, stirring the peace of the cabin's confined space, while Ruby perched on the arm of the settee. They both glanced up expectantly when she entered the room.

"Thanks for coming to help move Alex's things over," Jann said, "but I might not be going on the shoot after all."

"What do you mean, girl?" Capt'n demanded, abruptly ceasing his pacing. "Why aren't you going?" His bushy brows drew together, and beneath them his eyes pierced hers.

"Hush, Capt'n," Ruby admonished. "What is it, Jann? Has

Peter been giving you problems?"

"When hasn't he?" Jann asked wearily. "But this is nothing I can blame on him."  She met Ruby's gaze and knew, when the older woman's eyes widened, that her own concern was evident on her face.

"Alex is sick," she continued briskly. "He's hot, his nose is running, and he looks downright miserable."

"The little beggar probably got too much sun," Capt'n said ferociously, hiding his worry, Jann could tell, behind his bluster. "I warned you he needed a hat yesterday, girl."

"Let's have a look at him," Ruby said, shooting a repressive glance at her husband.

Alex was awake again by the time they'd all crowded into the tiny fore-cabin.

"Doesn't look sick to me," Capt'n muttered. "Women," he spat, "getting into a tizzy over nothing."

Ignoring him, Ruby lifted Alex out of his cot and carried him through to the main cabin. Jann's throat was tight as she watched the older woman put her hand to the baby's forehead.

"He is warm," Ruby agreed, then she cast Jann a reassuring smile. "But not overly so."  Peering down at Alex's drooling mouth, she gently inserted her little finger between his lips. "Swollen," she pronounced, as she felt his gums. "I thought as much."

"What is it?" Jann asked, catching a breath and holding it.

"Well, speaking as a nurse with over forty years experience . . ."  She grinned broadly, then assumed a learned expressed. ". . . I'd say, he's teething."

"Teething!" Jann exclaimed, disgusted with herself.

Ruby chuckled. "Don't worry about it, honey. Even seasoned moms get fooled. Just give that baby to us and you go off and enjoy yourself."

"I'm not going on vacation," Jann protested. "I'm there to work."

"We can manage a bit of both, don't you think?"

Jann spun around. Peter stood on the stairs behind her, his eyes very light this morning, and shining, as though from excitement. Anticipation shot through nerve-endings already taut with anxiety, anticipation she'd have to resist, along with the man himself. Despite the fact they were adversaries, she was attracted to him. And that had to stop. All he cared about was Alex and taking her baby from her.

Jann shifted her gaze from the setting sun and watched as Peter uncorked a bottle of chilled Chardonnay. A spattering of goose bumps erupted on her arms. Her boat had seemed much larger in port, her plan of keeping her distance from Peter more possible. Here at sea, it was excruciatingly apparent what a tiny space they were in, and that within its limited confines, they were alone.

Splashing some wine into two glasses, Peter handed one to her.

"How long will it take us to get to Maui?" he asked.

"Most of the night." She took a sip of her wine, not wanting to think about the night or her awareness of Peter Strickland.

"You've got it on self-steering now?"

"Yes. Unless we get a change in the wind or some marine traffic, it'll be fine like that until dark."

"Which watch would you like me to take?"

She looked up at him, surprised. "I wasn't expecting you to take a watch."

"Were you planning to do everything yourself?"

"I don't need any help."

"Then why am I here?"

"I . . ."

"I'll take the first four hours," he suggested, "you take the second, then I'll be on again 'til morning."

"Who do you think you are?" she flared. "I don't even know if you can trim the sails, let alone steer. I have no intention of entrusting my boat to a novice!"

"I'm no novice," he said quietly, raising his hand to stop her as she opened her mouth to speak. "Which is why I've allocated myself the first shift. That way, you'll be able to see for yourself." He held out one hand, palm upturned. "Fair enough?"

Her mind racing, Jann reluctantly nodded.

"Good." Peter clinked his glass against hers. "Let's drink to it."

Darkness had closed around them like the arms of a lover, the water rolling beneath the keel as ageless as all eternity. Watching Peter at the wheel from her place in the cockpit, Jann felt strangely at peace. Men and women had been riding the sea for centuries and would no doubt still be doing so long after she and Peter had said their final good-byes.

She stared thoughtfully out over the black water. Peter was a good sailor, for which she was more than a little grateful. Steering all night, then working the next day would have been difficult. If they had got away more quickly from Honolulu it wouldn't have been necessary, but last minute chores had positively eaten up the hours.

"Made a wish?" Peter asked softly.

"I beg your pardon?" she said, turning to him.

"Shooting star," he said, motioning toward the sky. "Didn't you see it?"

She leaned against the pillow she'd propped behind her back and stared up at the heavens.

"You don't usually see them this early in the evening," she said. "But then again, you can see much more clearly out here than in the city."

"I know what you mean."

His voice sounded so strange, she glanced at him again. He was looking down at her, but against the dark sky she couldn't see his face properly. Her stomach muscles tightened. Impossible to tell what he was thinking.

"What did you wish for?" he asked softly, his voice at odds with the hard line of his jaw.

"Nothing," she replied briskly, too aware of him here in the dark. "I didn't see it." It was the way he stood—so easily, so powerfully—the way his arms had felt when he pulled her to him—the way his lips thrilled hers.

She blinked and shook her head. Images thrust up by the night. Mirages, nothing more.

"Where did you learn to sail?" she asked, struggling to divert her thoughts from those she couldn't afford.

"My father," he answered, adjusting the wheel to starboard a fraction of an inch. "Sometimes when he was home, we'd mess about in boats."

Jann's throat tightened. She'd spent hours with her father, also, fishing, playing catch . . . .

"We started with a raft on the back pond at Willow House." Peter chuckled, a reminiscing, happy sound. "My father said we'd graduate to something larger when I understood the water from the fishes' point of view. He made me dive off the raft and float around in the current, assessing which way the raft would drift."

Picturing him there, Jann liked what she saw. "And did you figure it out?" she asked.

"Not really. It was just my father's way of making sure I was comfortable in the water. He didn't want me to underestimate it. He believed if you could recognize the dangers on a pond, you would understand your vulnerability on the ocean. He wanted me never to have an inflated sense of myself."

Laughter peeled from Jann's throat, startling even her in the still night air. Peter was looking at her as though she had suddenly gone mad, but it was impossible to choke back another bout of giggles.

"And did he succeed?" she finally managed to ask, wiping her hand across watering eyes. "In making you suitably humble, I mean?"

"Let's just say, I respect the ocean," he answered, grinning back at her.

"What happened next?" she asked, still chuckling. "Did you graduate to a dinghy?"

"Better than that. We went out on a Flying Junior—a two-man sailboat—for a couple of months. The yacht club we belonged to rented them out to members."

Yacht club. A different world from the one in which she'd grown up.

"Of course, we often went out in our own boat. But he wouldn't let me sail alone. Not until I'd earned the right." He gave her a swift look. "That's one thing I respect him for. People have to earn what they get. Nothing comes free."

Jann's smile died. Not even Alex. To get him, she had lost Claire. With a shiver, she reached for her sweater and pulled it around her shoulders.

"You must miss your father," she said quietly. Strange to think he'd experienced the same pain as she. "Your mother, too, of course."

The moon came out from behind a cloud and cast a light over Peter's face. But he turned away and stared out to sea, his face again now lost in shadow.

"Of course." His voice had hardened, seemed filled with an anger denying his words. "But she didn't have much time for me. Or for Claire." He faced her again, his expression grim. "Or for my father in the last few years before they died."

Jann's lips trembled. Her own parents had been so different. Always laughing, always touching, brimming over with a happiness that seemed invincible. Only it hadn't been, and that was her fault. She clutched her sweater more tightly, her chill deepening.

"Hey . . ." Peter moved beside her, his strong fingers cupping her chin. ". . . don't worry about me," he said gruffly. "I gave that up years ago."

Staring into his eyes, she read the truth. "You don't just forget your childhood," she protested. She never wanted to lose her memories of the time before her parents died. It was all she had left.

"You do if you're smart," he said, looking as though he meant to touch her, perhaps kiss her, but was fighting that impulse. At the last instant, he returned to his place at the wheel.

"What was your mother like?" she asked, curious.

He shrugged, but the rest of his body turned stiff.

"You don't talk about her," Jann persisted.

"Nothing I want to say." He shrugged again. "She was beautiful," he added softly. "Had Claire's eyes, Claire's hair—"

"Yours too," Jann said, smiling.

". . . and she smelled like flowers." His body relaxed. It seemed as if he were talking to the heavens now, for he wasn't looking at her, didn't seem connected to the boat or the earth at all.

Jann's mother had smelled wonderful, too, like homemade baking and steaming hot chocolate.

"People were attracted to her," Peter went on, "though men more than women. Even when I was a little kid, I could see that much." He frowned. "My father didn't like it, but there was nothing he could do. Trying to tie down my mother was like trying to catch a butterfly."

His eyes darkened. "She used to laugh at him when he tried to tell her what to do. She was always laughing." His voice lowered. "When I was little I used to feel nothing could go wrong as long as she was around."

"And when you were older?" Jann whispered, barely daring to speak, afraid that if she did, he would hold it all in.

"She wasn't around much." His face closed over.

"Where was she?"

"Rock concerts, parties, jaunts over to Europe."

"With your dad?"

"No." Peter's lips twisted. "My dad wasn't interested in that seventies stuff. He was too busy making money. My mother used to tell him to chill out, that he was an old fuddy-duddy working all the time. But he didn't like her friends, didn't want anything to do with drugs and the counter-culture."

"That wasn't all the hippie scene was about."

He looked at her, and his gaze seemed to burn.

"There were good things too," she went on hurriedly, "like protests, and peace movements, and—"

He laughed, the sound of it slicing the still air like a knife. "My mother wasn't into the politics of the thing. She just wanted the excitement, wanted to get away. From us," he added bitterly. "Claire and me."

Jann leaned towards him, wanted to take him into her arms and wipe the pain from his eyes. "I can't believe . . ."

"Believe what? That a mother would do such a thing?"

"Yes," she said softly.

"My mother did." His jaw line tightened. "She liked us well enough when it was convenient." His voice was tight also. "But we were in the way." He pulled in a deep breath. "Which is why I promised myself I would never make the same mistake."

"What do you mean?"

"Fall in love, get married."

Jann's heart contracted. His pain was so tangible, she could almost touch it.

"At least not to a woman like my mother," he went on.

She saw in his eyes with a clarity that seared, that he thought she was like his mother, a flaky, pleasure-seeking woman with no more real emotion than the butterfly she resembled.

"You can't hang on to your childhood forever," she said furiously.

"I agree," he said politely, "but I can learn from it."

"So what about Alex?"

"What about him?"

"If you get custody of him, how will he fit in?"

"He'll fit in fine." Peter's eyes filled with certainty. "We'll move into Willow House. It has a big garden Alex can play in, and a stone wall surrounding the property. He'll be safe."

Perspiration formed between Jann's shoulder blades, and a film glazed her eyes, as never-ending stone walls marched through her brain like soldiers. Walls with no gates. Walls holding her hostage. No matter how much she had wanted to leave, the walls hadn't let her, the courts hadn't let her, either, though no one really cared she was there. Certainly not Matron with her starched white dress and unsmiling eyes.

"I've already spoken to Claire's old nanny," Peter continued. "She's agreed to come back and help care for Alex as she did Claire. She's looking forward to it."

Jann's breathing seemed to cease. She couldn't let this happen. Not to Alex. She couldn't let him go to Willow House with its walls and nanny.

"What's the matter?" Peter demanded. Reaching forward, he touched her gently on the shoulder, bringing her back to her boat and the clear night sky. "You're shaking."

"I'm fine." She had asked him about his parents but she could never tell him about hers, about them dying, or about the orphanage. Not now. Not ever. He would only find some way to use it to his own advantage.

"Why didn't you finish your education in Boston?" she

asked instead, steering the talk away from Alex and the sort of life he would lead with Peter as his father. Her question sounded ridiculous, like meaningless chitchat at a cocktail party, but she had no choice.

Peter's eyes narrowed, and for a long moment, he simply looked at her.

Jann's gaze wavered, and she tucked her hands in the sleeves of her sweater so he wouldn't see them tremble. He must know she was hiding something, that her change of topic had been deliberate.

"Why Cambridge?" she added, desperate to fill the silence.

"My father wanted me to go there," he responded, at last, but he still watched her, reduced her to immobility.

A steady pain pounded her temple.

"He felt the contacts I made in England would be useful for business." Unexpectedly, Peter grinned. "He was right. Better than that, I enjoyed myself. Made some close friends. Felt at home."

"And after you graduated?" She could barely wrap her tongue around her words, but the questions were coming easier now. It stunned her how much she cared, how much she wanted to know more about him.

"I came back to the States to take my father's place in the company." His lips twisted. "My uncle wasn't keen on that idea."

"Did he have a choice?"

"Not really." Determination marked his face. The same determination his uncle must have seen. "But I did, and I decided I didn't want the job." He drew in a deep breath. "So I left."

"You make it sound so simple."

"Sometimes things are simpler than they look. I felt as though nothing more could touch me, as though I'd been through the wars and come out alive. Invincible.

Superhuman."

"I've never felt like that," she whispered. "It must be wonderful."

He leaned towards her then as though he meant to kiss her, and she leaned forward, too, pulled to him despite her fears.

"So you went traveling?" she asked, forcing herself to back away, trying not to watch his lips and dream of them on hers.

"Not right away," he answered slowly. "I had to decide what I wanted to do about my father's business first. In the end I sold my share to my uncle. Claire sold hers, too, when she came of age." His expression hardened. "She didn't get much use out of her money."

"And you?" She didn't want to speak of Claire. Not tonight.

"I traveled." His expression brightened. "I saw things, incredible things—people, cultures . . ." He paused again. ". . . and most especially, the things they create to make their lives endurable."

His hand swept the air. "Strickland's Import—Export Ltd. was born," he said, grinning. "I made a hell of a profit."

"You can pretend it was for the profit," she said softly, "but you're not fooling anyone."

"Aren't I?" he asked.

"No," she said, meaning it. She had seen what was in his eyes, heard what was in his voice. He had respected the people he met, admired them. A warmth stole over her, a dangerous warmth. Abruptly, she stood.

"I'm going to bed," she said. "Wake me at midnight."

Jann pulled the cotton quilt higher and tried to sink into her mattress, but was unable to fall back to sleep. It was too bright somehow, long past the time to get up. Why hadn't Alex wakened her?

Alex! Her eyes snapped open. Then realization set in and

she relaxed back into the warm grove her body had made against her sheets. Alex was with Ruby and John, and she was here—with Peter Strickland. Which was why she had barely slept.

She had tossed and turned in her bed until midnight, until it had actually been a relief to go back on deck for her watch. At least then she hadn't had to pretend to herself she was sleeping. But it had been equally impossible to sleep when her watch was over. Just knowing Peter was on the deck above her disturbed her somehow.

With a sigh, she pressed her eyes shut, attempting for what seemed the hundredth time to relax her muscles enough to sleep. She breathed in long, slow breaths. Peter had been different last night—slowly, breathe slowly—more open, somehow. She mustn't move. If she kept shifting around, she would never drop off.

She must have slept, for suddenly, she was as certain Peter was in the cabin with her as she was that losing Alex would mean her end. Her limp limbs reformed rigidly while slowly . . . ever so slowly, she opened her eyes.

Peter stood propped against her door, his shock of black hair disheveled from the night wind. Rising onto one elbow, Jann shook her own hair back from her face.

"You awake?" he asked softly.

"Yes," she replied dazedly, her brain fuddled with fatigue. "What time is it?"

"Eight o'clock."

"How long have you been standing there?"

"Not long." He smiled slowly, a buccaneer with his black woolen sweater and early morning stubble.

He had been watching her sleep! Her cheeks flared hot. "Don't worry." He grinned cheekily. "You didn't talk in your sleep or snore."

Glaring at him, she pulled the blanket higher. "Why aren't

you at the wheel?"

"I left it on self-steering for a few minutes." He gazed around her cabin, his scrutiny catching everything. He even glanced at the framed picture she kept on the shelf next to her bunk.

"Your parents?" he asked.

"Yes," she answered stiffly. The picture had been taken a few months before they died.

Peter was looking at her, an unspoken question in his eyes. But after last night, she couldn't talk of her parents to Peter. Knowledge was power and he had enough of that already.

"What are you doing in here?" she demanded. Her cabin felt too small, her bunk too big.

"You asked me to wake you. Remember?" He picked up a miniature vial of perfumed oil from her dresser, pulled out the stopper, and sniffed appreciatively. "It's been a pleasure," he added, bestowing on her another grin.

"Well, I'm awake now," she muttered, more heat spreading from her neck to her face.

"I can see that."

"So go. I need to get dressed."

He re-stopped the essence and put it back on her dresser. "Pretty," he said, almost to himself, almost as though he meant her, not the oil. "Take your time," he added, giving her one last inscrutable glance before turning and striding out the door.

Jann hurriedly pushed back her quilt and struggled to her feet. She tugged on her shorts and a clean tee shirt and headed toward the main cabin. Putting the kettle on to boil, she pulled two mugs from the cupboard and placed them on the galley's narrow counter. Then, sinking onto the settee, she balefully eyed the mugs.

Still two nights left. The worst of it was that at times during the previous night, she'd actually liked Peter Strickland.

More than liked, if she was honest.

She shook her head, hoping the movement would wipe those fancies from her mind. She couldn't afford to like Peter. It was too dangerous already that she was taking the risk with Alex.

Besides which, when Peter talked about his mother, he made it perfectly clear that he thought Jann was just like her, a woman who played at being a mother, but when things got inconvenient would throw in the towel.

It hurt that he thought that, but she couldn't let herself be hurt. To ensure custody of Alex, she had to remain on guard, couldn't let the man who wanted her baby get under her skin. Peter Strickland was capable of anything if it got him what he wanted. By the cold, clear light of morning, that much was clear.

Her fingers curled into a fist. She had to continue to see things clearly, to keep strictly business her relationship with Peter Strickland, to put a halt to this unfortunate habit they'd fallen into of discussing their personal lives. She couldn't need, couldn't want to know what he'd been doing for the past ten years.

Couldn't afford to know.

Filled with new resolve, she moved back into the galley where she swiftly made toast and fried two eggs. She shuddered at the sight of them lying on the plate, and reached into the wire basket hanging from the ceiling. Extracting an orange, she popped it into her shorts' pocket, then loading everything else onto a tray, she carried it up on deck.

"Come and get it," she said briskly. "I'll steer."

"Aren't you eating?"

"Of course." She pulled out her orange and peeled it, then moved to take his place at the wheel. "Now eat. We've got a big day ahead of us."

"Which is why you need more for breakfast than an

orange." He eyed her critically. "It looks like I'll have to take you in hand."

"What do you mean?"

"Tomorrow morning . . ."

She held her breath.

". . . I'll make you my world famous whole wheat banana pancakes."

Her breath escaped in a whoosh.

"Guaranteed to make even the staunchest health nut whimper for more."

"We'll see about that," she said, a smile tickling her lips.

"There! Do you see it?" Jann shouted.

Peter came up behind her, his body separated from hers by only a hand's width. She could still feel his heat. Goose bumps rose on her arms then skittered across her shoulders.

"There," she said again, pointing, fighting an inexplicable urge to lean back against him. "On the horizon."

"How do you know it's one of the racers?"

"I just do!" she exclaimed, excitement claiming her.

"Women's intuition?"

"If you like." She glanced around at him, his green eyes disconcertingly close. "It seldom fails me," she added, smiling.

"Run with it then." He smiled back at her and leaned closer. "Just remember to listen carefully when it tells you things your head can't accept."

"Such as?" she demanded.

His smile broadened to a grin. "You figure it out."

"I need to set up my cameras," she said briskly, trying to shake off the tentacles of warmth overtaking her. "Can you maneuver us into position?"

"I'll be ready when you are." He moved to trim the sails, then glanced back at her, his eyes serious. "They'll be good, you know—your pictures, I mean."

His enthusiasm was catching. Suddenly anything seemed possible, which was how life should be. A job she loved, sunshine all around, and the right person with whom to share it.

Her skin rippled with new shivers. It was happening again. Peter Strickland was casting a spell and reeling her in. She had to resist, had to focus on her photography, nothing else. If she could capture this race, the thrill and disappointment of it, then she'd really have something to sell! Then she could provide for Alex without touching his trust fund.

Peering toward the horizon, she saw not one boat, but two. Adrenaline whistled through her, as exhilarating as a stiff breeze on a hot day. She had prayed for a tight finish but hadn't believed it would really happen.

The boats were so close it was difficult to distinguish one from the other. Like prehistoric mating birds, their sails dipped and bobbed in unison.

Then she glanced toward the Maui coastline. Small dots, growing larger by the moment, were heading out to meet the racers who had traveled thousands of miles to the finish.

But she would be there first! She would get her pictures before the local boats even got close. Excitement surging through her, she pushed her cameras into a corner of the cockpit and reached for the wheel. Peter stood at the mast, legs spread, rolling with the movement of the boat as he trimmed the sails.

When he was done, he moved closer, his cat's eyes gleaming. "Are you ready? They'll be on us in seconds."

Jann nodded. Relinquishing the wheel to Peter, she picked up her cameras and moved to the bow of the boat. The view was perfect. She harnessed her camera bag to the anchor winch, then crouched beside it. Raising her camera to her eye, she trained it on the swiftly approaching sail boats. She wouldn't use the tripod. Though Peter would keep the boat as motionless as possible, with the rolling of the sea the camera would be steadier in her hand.

The racers were closer now. Jann began to snap pictures, close-ups with one camera, the broad view with another.

She was near enough now to see the crews on both vessels, the sailors' faces pinched from an exhausting two weeks at sea. They seemed oblivious to everything but their assigned jobs.

But occasionally, for an instant only, the cautious masks shrouding their faces dropped, and glimpses of elation showed through. Their prayers, that theirs would be the first boat over the finish line, sparkled from each sailor like star bursts from heaven.

Virtually neck and neck, the racers swept towards *HEART'S DESIRE*, a tail wind filling their spinnakers. Peter kept a tight grip on the wheel of Jann's boat, holding it all but stationary, but she could see his gaze locked on the racers, his lips curving into a smile.

The racers were in line with them, when suddenly, inexplicably, the wind changed direction, coming from behind *HEART'S DESIRE* now and across the racers' decks. The craft closest to them harnessed the breeze and the crew scrambled to new positions as the vessel heeled to one side. Then it flew like a hawk ahead of the other boat.

Jann continued snapping photos, first of one crew then the other, still close in distance, but miles apart in expression. On the one shone victory, on the other, defeat. Then suddenly, as though they had never been there at all, both boats were gone, bearing toward the shore and the crowds lining the dock.

Jann sank breathless against the bow's railing, resting a moment before slowly gathering her cameras and clambering back along the narrow deck to the stern. The racers were far ahead now, removed from her physically, but their spirit still hung like a rainbow in the air.

"Well?" Peter asked, his gaze meeting and holding hers.

"Yes!" Jann said softly, exultation sweeping through her.

Then, "Yes," she said again, louder this time.

He held out his arms.

For the space of a heartbeat, she hesitated, as a swimmer would before a dive. Then with a cry, she threw caution aside and plunged, falling into Peter's arms as though she belonged.

# Chapter Ten

A current as binding as the circle of Peter's embrace surged between them. Though Peter's body shielded Jann from the wind's full force, it caressed her skin as she linked her fingers at the base of his neck.

The breeze buffeted his hair forward, covering eyes that reflected her own joy. Then slowly, inevitably, he captured her mouth with his.

She froze for one long uncertain moment, then, like an icicle in late spring, she thawed beneath his heat. His lips were as salty as the sea breeze itself, yet as variable as the ocean. Firm and unrelenting one moment, the next yielding to the contours of her mouth.

One kiss formed another, then went on to another. Had there been a beginning? She no longer knew. Her swollen lips searched for his, wanting him. Wanted as she couldn't want. Needed as she couldn't need. With a mighty effort, she turned away. As he turned away, also.

"We decided not to do this anymore," she said, amazed she could sound so definite.

"We did," he agreed hoarsely.

She ran her tongue over her lips, still able to taste him, still wanting him. Trembling, she faced him again, piercingly aware of every line and plane of his face, every shade of color in his eyes. Impossible to draw away, impossible to be so near. She stepped backward, her heels banging hard against the solid side of the cockpit.

His gaze searched hers.

"It complicates things," she went on, lifting her chin higher, firming her jaw.

"There's nothing simple about it," he agreed, touching her arm.

"I'm attracted to you," she admitted, her throat suddenly dry, not able to now deny the feelings surging through her. "But that's as far as it goes."

As far as she could risk letting it go.

"You're afraid," Peter accused.

She was afraid. Afraid of Peter and how he made her feel. The sort of feeling that could end in just one way.

Pain.

She knew about pain, knew nothing was worth that.

Except Alex.

"Are you afraid of what you're feeling?"

She couldn't answer him that.

"Or of change?"

"Nothing's going to change."

"Or of me?" he finished softly.

His question pierced Jann's heart.

An unfathomable expression clouded his eyes.

Was he regretting the kiss already?

So why had he kissed her? And so passionately? Her heart shriveled. Was it to gain custody of Alex? The one thing she couldn't afford to lose and the one thing Peter was prepared to go to any lengths to get.

She tore her gaze from his and stared out to sea. "You're on this boat, don't forget, because I need your help."  With a struggle, she steadied her voice. "And because you're killing time until you can see Alex again. Let's not make this situation worse than it already is."

"Nothing could make it worse."  Cupping her chin in his hand, he pulled her around to face him. "There is a solution," he said softly. "Don't fight me on Alex and we'll take it from there."

Pain stabbed her lungs, snatching at her breath and scattering it to the winds. When she pulled in another, salty air stung her throat. "That's not a solution," she answered, not wanting Peter to see her hurt. "That's an impossibility."

Jann stepped into the phone booth in front of the drug store and drew the door shut. Rummaging in her purse for some coins, she dropped them in the slot.

"Hello," Ruby answered, her cheerful voice warbling down the line.

"Hi, Ruby. It's me. We made it. How's Alex?"

"He's fine." Her friend chuckled. "He and John are sound asleep on the couch. John was supposed to be entertaining him while I made dinner."

The corners of Jann's lips tugged upward. Not the first time the Capt'n's endless stories had put someone to sleep.

"Did you make good time?" Ruby asked, her question drawing Jann's attention back to their conversation. "No problems along the way?"

"No." Jann's smile died. "No problems." Not if you discounted impossible feelings for a man who could give her nothing, yet wanted everything she had and then some. She cleared her throat. "Has Alex's temperature gone down?"

"He's still a little warm . . ."

Jann's fingers tightened around the receiver.

". . . but I think I felt the edge of a tooth this morning."

Her grip eased.

"As soon as it's through, he'll be right as rain. How's Peter?"

Jann's throat grew constricted. She couldn't reply.

"Is he behaving himself?"

"What do you mean?"

"I guess if you don't know," Ruby replied, her laughter splashing through the line over her, "then he is. Too bad. I had great hopes for that young man."

"Ruby, really!" Her friend was incorrigible! She would have to be set straight before her imagination got completely out of hand. Jann glanced out the phone booth window.

Peter's legs were all that remained visible beneath the low hanging roots of the banyan tree dominating the town square. She turned her back on him, determined to ignore the tingle the sight of him always brought, trying, instead, to concentrate on her conversation.

"Peter isn't interested in falling in love," she reminded her friend.

"Men seldom are," Ruby said. "Luckily, they seldom see it coming."

"We can't even be friends, let alone more than that. I don't like the man." She swallowed hard on the lie. "Or trust him. There's only one thing on his mind, and that's to take Alex away."

"Jann, honey——"

"There's nothing more to say about it."

"I've seen the way he looks at you," the older woman countered softly.

Jann caught a swift breath, then released it slowly before speaking. "What way?"

"As though he doesn't want to like you any more than you want to like him, but he can't help himself." Ruby's voice held more amusement. "It seems to make him testy."

"He's testy, all right."

"He's not the only one," her friend chided gently.

Jann rested her forehead against the cool glass of the phone booth, grateful Ruby couldn't see her face. "I have to go now," she said hurriedly. "We're going out for a quick bite, then back to the boat to bed."

"That sounds more promising."

"Ruby," Jann protested, then stopped, defeated. It was no use. She knew Ruby too well. Her friend would never let up 'til Jann was married and had six kids. Well, it would be a snowy day in Hawaii before that happened!

"Give Alex a kiss for me," she murmured softly, a sudden

longing to hold her baby sweeping up and overwhelming her. "Take good care of him."

"You know I will. Cheerio," came Ruby's cheerful reply, then she hung up on her end.

Temples throbbing, Jann slowly placed the receiver back on its hook. Ever since Peter had kissed her, the day had gone wrong. Not talking further, they had silently followed the lead boats into Lahaina and anchored *HEART'S DESIRE* in the harbor. They'd rowed into shore in the dinghy, all the while keeping warily apart from one another, as though engaged in an uneasy truce, as though something could erupt at any moment.

All afternoon, she had snapped photos of triumphant sailors and cheering onlookers, shifting at times to capture the disappointed faces of the men and women on the boats finishing too late to be first.

She had caught glimpses of Peter as she worked, his black head rising above the crowd and drawing her eye as a magnet draws metal, until, at last, he had disappeared, leaving her in what she thought would be peace.

But it hadn't worked out that way. Even with him gone, she hadn't been able to concentrate. Jann frowned. The pictures she'd taken on shore would be mediocre at best, technically competent but lacking the emotion and perspective she had managed on the water. It would be a miracle if she could salvage any that were decent.

She glowered in the direction of the banyan tree. Peter might be made of money, but she wasn't! To survive, she had to sell her photos.

Peter was completely visible now. He had dropped down out of the tree's enormous low-lying branches and was lounging against the trunk looking far more comfortable than he had any right to look.

Jann strode across the street, dust spiraling up from

beneath her feet. But when she shoved aside a trailing root of the banyan, she halted, suddenly hesitant. The ethereal atmosphere of the enclosed space beneath the tree's branches evaporated the hard edge of her annoyance, and the sunlight filtering in through the filigreed roots was magical.

"You spoiling for a fight?" Peter drawled.

Jann blinked, the spell broken.

"Or have you run out of film?" His gaze drifted over her face.

"No," she snapped.

"Then it must have been the phone call."

He had seen her as clearly as she'd seen him.

"You called Ruby," he guessed correctly. "Is Alexander all right?"

"Nothing's wrong."

"Then it's something else that's eating you."

"You know very well what the problem is!"

"You're not still worried about that kiss?"

"No," she lied. "As long as we're clear about it never happening again." With her skin already broiled by the sun and sea breezes, perhaps he wouldn't notice the heat sweeping her face.

"Come along," he said, drawing close and taking her by the elbow. He pulled her after him through the dangling roots.

"Where are we going?" she demanded, digging in her heels.

"We've got a reservation for dinner."

"I'm not hungry."

"You soon will be." He moved off again with a gentle tug on her hand. "You don't eat enough to keep a fly alive."

"I was planning to have dinner on the boat." She felt breathless with the sudden movement, or maybe it was the way he held her by the hand.

"A romantic dinner for two?" he asked, with a backward glance towards her. He smiled. "Sounds good."

"I was thinking more of a sandwich for one. I wouldn't dream of holding you back from a night on the town."

He suddenly pulled her hard against his chest, ignoring her gasp of protest. A middle-aged woman and her balding counterpart, clad in twin Hawaiian-print shirts, passed slowly by on the narrow sidewalk.

Peter's body shaped to hers, fitting spoon-like against her back like it had once before. Only this time it was worse. His heat was her heat, too intimate, too intoxicating to ignore.

He held his arm across her chest just above her breasts. If she moved it would be as if he caressed them. Her nipples hardened and strained against her shirt.

The couple murmured, "Thank-you," as they passed, but Peter continued to hold her, a moment too long, a lifetime too short. It was as if she were paralyzed in a cocoon of heat. As his musky masculine scent tickled her nose, her hormones danced.

"Have you fallen asleep?" he whispered, his breath teasing her ear.

She attempted to move away, but his arms remained around her, keeping her close.

"If you're tired," he continued, his voice serious now, "I could take you back to the boat."

"No!" She pushed against his arm, until, with a suddenness that staggered her, he released her. "If I wanted to go back to the boat . . ." She turned and stared straight into his eyes. ". . . I am perfectly capable of getting there myself."

To spend an evening in his company, drawn to him but unable to act on those feelings would be difficult, but to be alone on the boat with him—she shivered—that would be impossible!

"But it has been a long day," she added. "I guess I'm hungrier than I thought."

He grinned down at her. "Right then," he said, holding out

his hand.

With reluctance, she took it, and together they wove between the tourists maneuvering the main street. The restaurant was down a narrow alley, half hidden by two potted palms standing sentinel-like on either side of a stained glass door.

The *maitre d'* led them to an inner courtyard complete with fish pond, splashing waterfall and intricately pruned bonsai trees. Their table stood in one corner, an elegant glass affair mirroring the garden's perfection.

"Like it?" Peter asked.

"Yes," Jann breathed, sinking into a cushioned wicker chair and scanning the courtyard with delight. "How did you discover it?"

"Contacts," he answered obliquely.

She frowned.

Peter chuckled, raising his hands in surrender. "While you were snapping your future fame and fortune . . ."

She stiffened. How had he guessed how much the photos meant to her?

". . . I was exploring. A fellow on the dock suggested this place. He said leave the harbor views and the mediocre food to the tourists." Peter grinned ruefully. "Mind you, he was pretty drunk."

She smiled back at Peter, his good humor infectious. An unfamiliar mixture of excitement and anticipation coursed through her.

"What would you like?" he asked, perusing the menu the waiter had left with them. "They seem to have every species of fish known to man."

She skimmed the bewildering list. "Alligator," she said at last, glancing up at him and smiling.

"Alligator!" His brows formed question marks, but a smile lurked on his lips.

"Something with bite." She grinned. "You never know

when you might need it."

Throwing back his head, he laughed out loud. Then he beckoned the waiter.

"Alligator for two," he ordered, a clear challenge in his eyes.

Jann accepted Peter's proffered hand and stepped off the dock into the skiff. She almost fell into Peter's lap, but he steadied her in the same way he steadied the boat, by holding on to her firmly.

Only with her it didn't work. She didn't feel steady at all. She had drunk too much wine, was feeling giddy with the effect. It had seemed appropriate at the time. Made her feel as though their having dinner together was somehow ordinary and safe—such as two friends might share. But now, sinking onto the skiff's wooden seat, willing the dizziness in her head to disappear, Jann wished she hadn't thrown caution to the wind.

Peter shoved an oar against the pier and pushed off, his muscles rippling as he rowed. The oars slipped through the water as noiselessly as thread through a needle, the only audible sound that of laughter echoing from harbor-side cafes.

It was impossible to avoid touching Peter, with his long legs stretched out on either side of hers. Warmly, seductively, they sent her nerve-endings into a tailspin.

She tilted her head back and gazed up at the stars instead. They usually offered perspective, but tonight they were no help. Even compared to the universe, her problems seemed as insurmountable as climbing a frayed rope to the moon.

She glanced down at her watch. Not even midnight yet. Late enough for bed, but—she glanced dubiously across at Peter—would she be able to sleep?

By the time they drew near *HEART'S DESIRE*, her stomach was in knots. Peter guided the skiff close to the ladder and she grabbed hold, teetering for an instant on the bottom rung before scrambling up. Peter tossed her the skiff's rope and she secured it to the boat.

Then he followed her up, his bulk looming black against the night sky as he stepped into the cockpit.

"Thank you for dinner," Jann said, struggling to slow the racing of her heart.

"My pleasure." His voice was as velvety as the night.

She shivered.

"Cold?" he asked, touching her shoulder.

"No," she gasped, heat racing through her.

"Don't worry," he said softly, moving inexorably closer. "I'm not going to kiss you again."

She wanted to be kissed. Her lips trembled with need.

His jaw was taut, his own lips tight with tension. And his eyes pulled her. For all their hooded intensity, they glowed— the kind of glow no woman could ignore.

He wanted her, and not just for a single kiss under a tropical moon, but completely. Possessively. Wholly. With nothing held back.

He wanted all of her.

Her lips parted. For an instant, she was positive he would take her right there on the deck, under the eyes of heaven.

And for that same single moment, she longed to take him in return. To give herself and be inflamed, to meet and match the thrust of his body and the penetration of his soul. To mingle their hearts and passion and come together as one. To be encircled in the shelter of his arms and loved as a woman should be loved.

As she never had been loved.

She saw all that was possible and ached to receive it, but this was the man who planned to take Alex from her. With an inarticulate cry, she pushed him away as fiercely as she would thrust a serpent from her bosom.

She wrenched the hatch open and hurtled down the

companionway. Through the chart room and main cabin, she came at last to the safety of her own bedroom. With a muffled sob, she flung herself onto her bunk, hot tears sliding down her cheeks and dampening her cotton sheets.

The great gulps of air she was pulling into her lungs suddenly became too much, and she calmed, regulating her breathing to a series of shallow gasps. Stilling herself as completely as she was able, she lay there and listened.

For what seemed an interminable length of time, she heard nothing save the slap of waves against the side of the boat and the creak of the anchor chain dangling from the hull.

Then she heard it. The muted sound of Peter's footsteps as he slowly descended the stairs. He approached her cabin, but for a long moment just stood there with no further sound. Then, without knocking, he turned from her door and away from her. The settee creaked, where earlier that evening she had left blankets for his bed.

Time passed but she was unable to relax. The face of her clock gleamed like a spotlight in the darkened room. First the seconds, then the minutes, then the half-hours trickled away, like sand through a sieve, never to return.

Staring into the blackness with burning eyes, Jann's mind spun like a whirligig in the wind. She was unable to settle, to allow sleep to rescue her.

She could think only of Peter, could imagine his hard, lean body crunched into the confines of the six foot settee, his cat's eyes glowing and restless in the dark.

Through the shadows, his soul called hers, stretching over the space between them and relentlessly willing her to come.

She clamped her eyes closed, but the images continued to flicker in her mind like flames within a pit, sometimes flaring up, and sometimes dampening down to embers, but always, always, hot.

She rolled over, tried to force her brain to visualize other scenes, other players. Anything to dispel the image of herself making wild and uninhibited love with the uncle of her son.

The night turned gray with early morning mist before finally she drifted, exhausted and confused, into a deep, dreamless sleep.

# Chapter Eleven

Tiny shafts of pain drummed through her skull, tapping a crescendo on the insides of her eyelids. Wincing, Jann opened her eyes to find sunlight streaking through a crack in her curtain and blazing across her face.

Morning.

She groaned. Time to get up. Twisting onto her side, she drew her knees to her chest.

Not yet. She couldn't face Peter yet.

How long do you think you can avoid him? an insistent voice nagged through the numbness surrounding her brain.

Forever would be just about right she silently answered back, then with a resigned sigh, straightened her legs and swung them over the edge of her bunk.

Wrapping her bathrobe around her, she slipped into the hall and swiftly made her way to the shower. The water streaming down her face felt good, but didn't pierce the fatigue cloaking her. She toweled herself dry, but even rubbing her body briskly couldn't make her forget the sleepless night she'd just passed.

Once back in her cabin, she sat motionless on her bed and tried to stop the swirling dizziness of her brain. But it was no good. No clarity emerged.

With a sigh, she leaned forward, disheveled curls tumbling across her face as she extracted a pair of purple shorts from the second drawer of her dresser. Streaking her hair back with her fingers, she tugged on the shorts then reached for her pink blouse.

After buttoning it, she sat motionless again, listening, as she had listened the night before. Nothing. Perhaps Peter wasn't awake yet. If he'd spent the same sort of night as she, he'd probably sleep until noon.

She stood, reluctant to look into the mirror above her dresser, and when she finally did, found her eyes were two black smudges of fatigue. Bruised and swollen from crying, they looked enormous on her pale face. She couldn't face Peter looking like this. He'd know in an instant he'd been the cause, would no doubt use it to his advantage.

She snatched a tube of lipstick, Cadillac Pink, from her top dresser drawer and drew a jaunty slash across her lips. Then she slathered make-up around her eyes and the worst of the night's ravages were subdued. The face staring from the mirror back at her wasn't perfect, but she'd do. Patched up, smoothed over, ready to face the world—Jann grimaced—or at the very least, one tall, handsome, too-dangerous-to-mess-with man.

She silently opened her bedroom door and tiptoed down the passageway toward the main cabin. Holding her breath, she peeked toward the settee.

Nothing.

Not one long leg dangling over the arm, not one muffled snore resonating from beneath the powder blue quilt.

Nothing.

Jann frowned. Where was Peter? She hadn't heard him leave.

Then she stepped into the cabin and the aroma of freshly brewed coffee hit her like a waft of perfume. He had been here, and not too long ago either. She cautiously moved into the galley, but other than the steaming coffee pot, there was no sign of him there either. She poured herself a cup of the black wake-me-up and made her way to the stairs.

Perhaps he'd had the decency to take himself off. She hoped so. It would give her time to collect her thoughts, to figure out how she was going to handle being around him for the next day and a half.

Shoving the hatch aside, she stepped outside and squinted into the morning sun, almost blinded as her eyes adjusted to the light. Blessedly warm right now, it would be a scorcher later on.

Peter watched her emerge and shade her eyes from the sun. He slung his wet towel around his neck, felt the water stream off his chest.

He could imagine how she would look in a bathing suit, had been imagining her naked all night long, had lain on the settee unable to sleep and unable to think beyond the consequences making love to Jann would incur.

"The water's great," he said, struggling to forget now all that had passed between them the previous night. "You going in?"

"A little early for me," she murmured, shifting her gaze to the water.

One part of him was relieved. When she looked at him with her big blue eyes, he desired her too much, wanted nothing more than to pull her down on the deck and kiss her until their problems disappeared.

"Plenty of time for swimming later," he said, "in Hana." Plenty of time to reduce his need for this woman to its proper place, to remember the difference between making love and being in love, to remind himself why he was in Hawaii in the first place.

"Hana?" she asked, looking up at him with a frown.

"I've always wanted to go there."

"Why?"

"To see the Seven Sacred Pools." If they could keep on the move, keep away from this boat, then perhaps he wouldn't need her so, wouldn't be making a list in his head of all the ways he was starting to like her. "We'll head out after breakfast."

"I'm not going to Hana. It's miles away."

"It's not so far." Was keeping her near him a bad idea, like placing a scotch in front of an alcoholic?

"I have a lot to do today," Jann protested.

"Until the dance this evening, you're free as a bird. You told me so yesterday."

"There are some boats not in yet. I was going to go back out."

"You don't need more pictures of boats!"  He took a step closer, unable to stop himself, unable to remember why he should. "What's the matter? Afraid to be alone with me?" His own heart thumped faster at the thought of being alone with her.

"Of course not," she said faintly, but her eyes were wide, as though she was as terrified as he.

"Good."  It was good. He'd be able to prove, if only to himself, that he didn't want her, didn't need her so much his body ached. "I arranged a car rental for today. We'll leave right after breakfast. I'll have you back in plenty of time for the Yacht Club dance."


Jann undid her seatbelt, let it swing back into its sprocket, then slowly pulled it out once more, this time making sure it didn't rest quite so snugly against her stomach. Peter did make the best banana pancakes she'd ever eaten, but they had left her so full she barely had room for air.

She glanced across at him. One hand rested lightly on the steering wheel while his other arm lay along the open window. He was obviously enjoying the low-slung sports car as much as she.

The way he'd been acting, the way he'd chatted all through breakfast about inconsequential events, it was as though last night had never happened, as though they were friends. Not almost lovers, not adversaries either.

There had been just that one moment, the merest flicker in his eyes, when she'd been certain he was about to say or do something, then the look had disappeared as though it had never been there at all.

Tomorrow they would sail home. She would see her baby. Be able to hold Alex and cuddle him, and know he was all right. She firmly squelched the now familiar thrust of anxiety, determined not to think about what Peter had said about access until he brought it up again. They understood each other better now. Perhaps he wouldn't bother to change a thing.

With a sigh, she returned her gaze to the road. They'd been climbing steadily for the past few minutes and with each ascending foot, her apprehension increased. She loathed hilly, cliff-side roads, had known the road to Hana lay along the shoreline, but somehow had imagined it to be flat. Level to the sea. Safe.

She sat up straighter, her fingers inching toward the loop of leather passing as a door handle. Then, with a suddenness that made her gasp, the next gentle bend twisted into a corkscrew. Straight ahead, all she could see was the azure blue of the sky.

The car clung to the road tenaciously, the cliff face along Jann's right side comfortingly solid. She stared past Peter and all thoughts of comfort vanished.

The ground fell away sharply at the edge of the road, dropping hundreds of feet over rocky outcroppings to the ocean below. Dizziness threatened to overwhelm her. She squeezed her eyes shut in an effort to control it.

"Are you all right?" Peter asked sharply, slowing the car to a stop. "Jann?"

She opened her eyes, reluctant to look in his direction, not wanting her gaze to stray past him to the nothingness of space.

He turned away from her, glanced toward the cliff edge instead. Her teeth caught her lower lip as she followed his gaze.

"You're afraid of heights," he accused, turning back to her again.

"I'm not," she muttered, pressing her lips tighter. But her fear reverberated like a bumper car at a fair.

"What, then?"

She didn't answer.

Peter shifted the car into gear, driving it off onto the road's shoulder, dropping in under the hill's shadow and jerking to a stop as far from the cliff edge as possible. With a swift turn of the key, with a shutter and a gasp, the car's engine died.

He gently pulled her around to face him. "What's the matter, Jann?" he asked again.

His eyes were insistent, their inky centers seeming to expand and whirl toward her, encompassing her, pulling her in as they had when he'd almost kissed her. But for some reason this time it felt all right.

More than all right.

Safe.

Her lips trembled. Nothing was safe. She'd felt safe that night with her parents also. She shut her eyes again, determined to block the pain.

Then he touched her. Just a simple brush of his fingers against her thigh, but the contact warmed her, made her believe she could tell him what had happened without it ripping her in two.

"It was on a road just like this . . ." She stopped, the effort to find the right words leaving her exhausted.

"On a road just like this . . . what, Jann?" Peter's voice had dropped to a silken caress, his eyes darkening to the color of the ocean at midnight—mysterious, enigmatic, yet infinitely soothing.

". . . that my parents died," she whispered. She glanced toward the cliff, but it was that other cliff she saw, where the sky wasn't blue, but rather black as a pit.

He slipped his arms around her and pulled her close, his heart now thumping comfortingly against her cheek.

For twelve long years she had kept the horror of her parents' death locked in her heart like poisonous waste in a vault, alternately ignoring it, then thinking about it, then trying once again to work it through in her mind. Despite all her efforts, she'd never managed to forget.

"Tell me," Peter commanded, his breath ruffling her hair.

Tell him that her parents' death had been her fault?

She could never tell him that.

He gently pushed her from him and held her so he could see her. She longed to shut her eyes, to block out the demand in his.

"How did they die?" he asked softly.

Few people over the years had even asked her that question, and those who had, had done so swiftly, not really wanting to know.

"We were on our way to the cabin we always rented at the lake." She didn't look at him as she spoke, found it easier that way. "It was my birthday. We were going to celebrate. My parents and I . . . we celebrated everything." Every day had been a party. Every moment a joy. But birthdays especially. A burning scorched her throat, as though a thousand tiny flames had been lit and flamed to life.

"How old were you?"

"Does it matter?" she asked wearily.

"Yes," he answered, his attention as relentless as sand blowing across a desert.

"Fourteen," she said, swallowing hard. "My friend Dale asked me to go to the theater with her and her family. I was thrilled. Thought it seemed very . . . grown-up."

"But you were headed towards the cabin?"

"That was later, after the theater." She looked at him then, found eyes soft with concern, tinged with an emotion she couldn't define.

Bewildered, she lowered her gaze. The top few buttons of

his shirt were undone, and wiry black hairs spiraled out through the opening. She longed to return her head to his chest, to block out the past and never examine it again.

"So you went with Dale and her family?"

"Yes," she said reluctantly, "My parents told me to go with Dale and enjoy myself, said it sounded the perfect birthday treat."

Peter's face was like marble, impassive, not moving.

"They went up to the cabin as usual, then came back for me Saturday evening when the play was over. They said we still had time to go to the cabin for a few days, so we headed back again that night." She was starting to feel dizzy again, as though no matter how many breaths she took, not enough oxygen found its way to her lungs.

She also felt chilled, as chilled as that night her parents had died.

"The road was icy," she said, glancing at the pavement in front of the car, "and narrow, like this road." Her lips felt frozen, too, like two blocks of ice sticking together.

"We went over the edge," she whispered, holding herself stiffly. Peter stroked her back in a long, caressing sweep, his fingers tracing a fiery path up her spine and across her shoulders, but the heat from his touch didn't penetrate her skin. She sat straighter yet, tried to hold onto her composure, tried to remain in control. . . unbreakable.

But no one was unbreakable.

Glancing back toward the cliff, she involuntarily clutched Peter's leg.

Falling, her stomach flying to her throat as it had when she was little, when her father had thrown her giggling and shrieking above his head. But this time, no one caught her. This time, she had landed. Not in a laughing tangle of arms and hair, cheek against cheek and warmth against warmth, but in a screaming, burning mass of metal against stone.

She would never forget the noise, or the terror in her mother's eyes as she wrenched her head around for one last helpless look, or the icy whiteness of her father's fingers as he fruitlessly clutched the steering wheel, twisting and turning it in a vain attempt to stop the car's headlong plunge.

But the silence that followed had been even worse. Complete. Absolute. Empty.

She had returned to consciousness yards from the burned-out wreckage of their car, flung from the back seat like a doll from a giant's hand. When she opened her eyes, she'd seen nothing at first, only the stars and the moon, and the black wall of the cliff. But when she twisted her head, the fiery ball that had been their car filled her heart and brain like a never-ending nightmare.

"They died," she said tonelessly, trying to shut out the images.

Peter stared down at her, his expression unchanged. No sign of horror, or even of pity. He stroked her hair now, his fingers tangling in its strands.

Numbness engulfed her once more. "It was my fault."

Peter's eyes grew black as shadows.

She pushed herself from him and huddled against the car door, the air surrounding her body as icy as her battered soul.

"It was an accident," Peter said firmly. His hand clamped her shoulder, as hot as the flat side of an iron. He dragged her around to face him. "Nothing to do with you."

"If I'd gone with them in the first place we'd never have been on the road that late at night." She pressed her lips closed, determined to keep them from trembling. "We'd never have been going back."

"You've been a mother now for months," he growled. "You know how demanding parenthood is. Your parents probably relished the opportunity to spend some time alone."

She knew all that, had been trying to convince herself for

years. "They made the trip back to town especially to get me!" she repeated dully. "If they hadn't, they'd be alive today."

"They could have died," he said, his words slow and distinct—compelling belief—allowing freedom from pain, "picking you up from school, or from the store, or from a friend's house. Or flying in a plane—like mine. They could have been killed crossing the street, for God's sake. Thousands are."

He made it sound so possible, made her want to believe.

"It's not your fault," he said gently, placing both hands on her shoulders. "Their fate had nothing to do with you."

His eyes had changed to the crystal green of a mountain lake. Their honest strength reached for her, loosening her despair and diluting it with acceptance, pushing it from her heart in wave after trembling wave.

He gathered her to his chest, the warm ballast of his arms stilling the tremors suddenly shaking her. Tears rolled down her face in unremitting currents, stretching the shackles binding her until some of them snapped, paving the way for healing.

Where her face lay, his shirt was damp. For a long moment she rested against him, drinking in his solace. Then gradually, so gradually it was all but unnoticeable, the pounding of his heart picked up speed, breaking through the stupor of her relief. It beat erratically at first, then raced so insistently her own heart matched its cadence.

Where her body touched his, her skin prickled with anticipation, became lit with the heat of a desire so intense, she moaned. As though sparked by the sound, heat flamed from him.

Her arms, motionless until now, disentangled themselves from his and stole upward until her hands joined around the back of his neck, the soft silk of his hair tickling her fingers.

"Peter," she whispered, struggling to remember he was the enemy, but unable to construct that image in the forefront of her mind. She was unable to think of anything, was able only to feel, relinquishing herself at last.

Peter's lips would heal. They descended towards hers slowly, compassion darkening his eyes to the color of a forest pool.

"Yes," she breathed, a sound as soft to her ears as the sigh of the wind.

He claimed her mouth and she shut her eyes, sinking beneath the wonder of his kiss. The taste, smell, and feel of him—all dazzled her senses and banished thought from her mind. Drowning in oblivion, she felt the moment could last forever.

Whoosh!

The car gave a violent shake. Fear jolted back as though it had never left. Unwilling to relinquish the touch of Peter's mouth, but needing to know the worst, Jann wrenched her lips from his and opened her eyes.

An enormous truck laden with lumber had thundered past them, the cavernous air tunnel it created rattling the car's windows and setting its body to vibrating.

It was as though she had been rattled, too, shaken by an external force to pull away from this man before it was too late.

"We'd better be going," she said hoarsely, loosening her grip from around Peter's neck.

He moved to kiss her again.

With difficulty, she averted her lips.

"Are you all right?" he asked softly.

"Yes," she lied, "but we should go . . ." She caught her breath. ". . . before it's too late."

"Too late for what?" he demanded huskily. "To hide what we're feeling?"

"Feeling?" she gasped, repeating the word helplessly. She couldn't allow herself to feel anything. This man had already succeeded in blurring what past experience had taught her— that love causes pain and was best avoided.

Love! Just saying the word sent a paroxysm through her chest and into her heart. She couldn't feel love for Peter. This was simply a physical reaction. Chemistry. Nothing more!

She tried to laugh lightly, as she'd seen other women do, but her effort ended in a croak, and appeared, if the rear view mirror was to be trusted, to be the falsest of smiles. She tried again, was more successful this time, her smile no longer a plastered-on parody of the real thing.

"I feel better," she said brightly, careful not to meet his eyes. "It's idiotic to be afraid of heights." She glanced at him then. "It was good of you," she began, her words stiffening as her body withdrew, "to be so sympathetic."

His lips, only seconds before moving wondrously over her own, were now a thin line. "We can't run away from the truth," he growled.

No, but she could damn well hide it from him.

"It has a way of catching up, whether we want it to or not".

She crossed her arms in front of her body, fending off the misery biting into her like hail.

With an angry movement, Peter pulled his arm from behind her back, reached for the car key, and turned it in the ignition.

# Chapter Twelve

Heat lines danced on the steep path in front of Jann, tugging and straining at the nerve endings behind her eyes. Or maybe it was the memory of Peter's too-perceptive gaze staring accusingly into her own that was making her head throb so unremittingly.

She carefully shut her eyes. If she did it slowly enough, maybe the pain would go away. It didn't. Bleakly, she opened them again. There was no point in being careful. The pain in her head might disappear, but not that other pain—the one stabbing into her chest like a knife.

Her heel hooked a root and she stumbled as the path wound its way through a grove of bamboo. The plants' leafy branches met overhead, swathing through the blanket of heat beating relentlessly down. An unexpected breath of cool air rose up from the earth, chilling the perspiration dripping between her breasts.

It might be cooler beneath the trees, but the tension crackling between Peter and herself was blistering. They had exchanged barely two words during the rest of the car ride and even now he walked ahead of her, his back ramrod straight.

"Let's head back," she suggested.

"No," Peter said stubbornly, turning to face her. "We're going to the top pool."

"Why? You can't possibly be enjoying yourself."

"The day has had its moments."

She flushed, trying to ignore the way her insides melted at the memory of his lips on hers.

"I want to show you the pools," he said again. His expression softened. "They'll be worth it," he promised.

"Don't you ever change your mind?"

"Never."

Jann's heart pounded. For a moment in that car, Peter's kisses had almost made her forget the reason he had come to Hawaii. She couldn't afford to forget. Tugging out the tail of her cotton blouse from the waistband of her shorts, she wiped her damp forehead.

Peter's shirt was damp, also. It clung to his body, outlining his broad chest and muscular shoulders.

"Let me take that," he offered, reaching for the camera case dragging down her left shoulder.

She shivered at the touch of his fingers on her bare skin, but beneath the goose bumps was heat—his heat. Her mouth turned dry as tinder.

He swung her camera bag over one shoulder, then reached toward her again. This time his hand trailed lightly down her arm, creating spirals of sensation along its path. When his fingers met hers, they closed around them gently.

"Come on," he said, giving her hand a tug, not seeming to notice the effect he had on her. "It isn't far now." Turning back to the trail, he half-pulled her up the slope behind him.

It would be easier to remember he was the enemy, Jann decided, if her knees didn't turn to jelly at his touch. If she let go of his hand, she might collapse, but by hanging on, she was equally lost.

As smoothly as rivers run downhill, Peter drew her up the path toward the uppermost pool. Sweating with exertion, they reached it at last, and standing together at the pool's edge, they watched as a waterfall spun out over the cliff in a silver strand before crashing to the rocks below.

Without a word, Peter handed her the camera case, anticipating her desire to capture the light-filled water forever. She worked mechanically at first, then with enthusiasm, but all the while she was aware of Peter, beside her, behind her, encircling her mind. When finally she was finished, she lowered her lens and faced him.

His face seemed naked somehow, as though all the emotion and tension had been filtered from it. His eyes were gentle as he gazed down on her, something indefinable lurking in their depths.

Reflected on their surface was a miniature rainbow that appeared, then disappeared, then reappeared again, as it did above the falling water.

"All done?" he asked, taking a step closer.

"Yes," she replied, spellbound by the colors dancing in his eyes. She cleared her throat. "It's beautiful here."

He smiled. "I've read about the upper pools, swore I'd visit them one day." Stepping past her, he moved to the very edge of the cliff.

A lump formed in her throat at the sight of him standing so near the precipice.

Then turning, he grasped hold of her hand. "Come stand by me," he said, drawing her forward. He pulled her around in front of him, his arms crossing her body.

She tentatively looked out over the edge, her gaze shying away from the drop below her feet. But with Peter holding her close, her fear dissolved, as fog does when the sun comes out.

"Magic," he murmured, his breath soft against her ear.

If he meant the sensations exploding through her body, she had to agree. His touch, his scent, produced a buoyancy so light she felt she might float away if he weren't hanging onto her so tightly.

"Unbelievable there's no one else here," she said, needing to say something lest she kiss him again.

"These upper pools are only for people who truly appreciate them. Special people."

"Are we special?" She twisted her head in order to see his face.

"Oh yes," he replied, his lips coming nearer. "We're special." His last words came out stiffly, as though he were trying as hard as she to ignore what was passing between them.

For one long dangerous moment, Jann stared into his eyes, then, with a gut-wrenching effort, she ducked from beneath his arms and moved away from the cliff, away from the danger of his arms, and back toward the safety of the pool. The water looked wonderful; clear, cold, and passion suppressing.

"I'm going for a swim," she said.

"We should be getting back. It's getting late."

Not back to that car, or that road, or that place where she had told him things she'd never told anyone. Before she risked that she had to rid herself of this heat, had to be able to sit next to him and not want him so desperately she burned.

Pleased that she had thought to change into her swim suit before they left Lahaina, Jann stripped off her shorts and top and stepped to the edge of the pool. She dove in, the chilly water robbing her lungs of air. But she went deeper, determined to dispel the need Peter aroused. Finally, her air all but gone, she re-surfaced.

"Looks cold," Peter said, his hands undoing the button on the waistband of his shorts, then moving toward the zipper.

"It is." Her brow puckered with the strain of keeping her gaze from his hands. She looked at his face instead, trying not to know he was unzipping his zipper. "But . . . refreshing," she croaked out, sighing with relief when he pulled off his shorts and revealed a slick black bathing suit underneath.

Discarding his shirt and shoes, he stepped toward the water's edge. When he dove in, he came up again in the middle of the pool, his face mere inches from her own. His eyelashes glistened with beads of water.

She paddled her feet furiously, vainly attempting to evade the forward propulsion of his body as he catapulted into her. Before she could twist to the side, their legs tangled, his skin slightly rough but unbelievably warm in spite of the cold water.

As though to steady himself, he touched her waist. But the current flowing toward the top of the waterfall forced her toward him. Her body bumped hard against his, his lean muscular lines meeting hers, pelvis to pelvis, chest to chest.

"Cooler now?" he whispered, the proximity of his lips creating a rippling current beginning at the base of her neck then streaking down her spine.

"Yes," she lied, heat racing through her body and burning its way up her throat.

Intending to push herself away, she placed her hands on his waist, but was no more successful at that than he had been. When her fingers met the slippery satin of his skin, she allowed them to rest there a moment, savoring the way his stomach muscles rippled.

Then the current buffeted her closer, making it impossible to achieve the leverage necessary to distance herself. Her right leg drifted between his legs, bringing her firmly up against the one part of his body she was most at pains to avoid. He tensed at her touch, his belly hardening beneath her fingers.

Jann shut her eyes, but not before she'd seen the naked desire in his, had seen something else there also. Determination? Uncertainty? Whatever it had been, it was not visible to her now. Waves of yearning coursed through her, turning her tangled limbs to rubber and her resolve to mush.

"Peter," she whispered, then found his mouth on hers, hard, insistent, and filled with fire. His tongue battered her lips, until, with a soft consenting moan, they parted. The floodgates of Jann's passion swung open, loosing unspent desires and allowing them to flow.

Breathlessly . . . expectantly, she listened for the voice of reason. Always, in the past, on the very few occasions she had allowed a man to be close, the voice had been waiting there, ready to stop her with a reminder that to love is to court disaster.

She had even made love—waiting for, longing for, that special moment when her body would take over from her mind and move of its own accord in passion's timeless dance.

But it had never happened.

It was as if her heart were frozen and along with it her soul. Her movements had always been mechanical, her embarrassment extreme. No cymbals crashed. No fireworks exploded.

There had been simply nothing.

If she couldn't feel, if she couldn't give, if she couldn't risk the loving because she might lose, then there was no point in trying.

But this moment was different—breathtakingly, brilliantly different. She struggled to remind herself Peter was the enemy, but that thought seemed to have no connection to this time or place.

As his tongue filled her mouth, a heady lust filled her senses. Her heart pounded faster, shifting from apprehension to desire. Her limbs loosened, and her muscles relaxed, her entire body giving itself up to pleasure. Relinquishing her fear, she allowed herself to feel, relishing the exquisite joy of sensation. Without a whisper, the voice of reason disappeared.

Peter's lips left hers, exploring the planes and contours of her face before traveling down the long curve of her throat. She drifted, her body entangled with his, the water buoying them up, undulating around and beneath.

His legs stiffened as he found his footing on the flat surface of a submerged boulder. He lifted her until her chest rose out of the water and her legs encircled his waist.

With an easy motion, as though making love were as natural as breathing, not the futile exercise it had been for her in the past, he unhooked the top of her bathing suit, eased it over her shoulders and let it float away, a fuchsia wisp against the water's clear blue surface.

His lips moved from the throbbing pulse at the base of her

throat to the glistening peak of her breast. His groan, the primitive sound of passion, quickened her blood to boiling. Encircling her nipple with his tongue, he kissed and caressed. Sensations rocketed through her, shaking her to her core.

He grasped her tightly within his arms, but she needed no encouragement to press closer. She desired nothing more than that his body be a wave, washing over, into, and through her.

She arched backward, her hands gripping his shoulders. Her breasts thrust toward him, allowing his lips easy access.

She could scarcely breathe.

She didn't need to breathe.

Desire sustained her more completely than air.

Her fingers kneaded his shoulders in rhythm with the thrust of his tongue against the hardened bud of her nipple, while involuntarily, her legs tightened around his waist.

With delicious slowness, he traced his way to the hollow between her breasts, then tantalizingly climbed up the other side. Her lips parted, her loins on fire.

His hands cupped her buttocks, pressing her closer, while his fingers slipped beneath the waistband of her suit, tracing a line of heat around its edge.

The air had turned still, as though nothing else existed. Or was it the pounding of blood through her veins that had blocked all other sound? The warble of a songbird brought the world into focus, but even that sweet sound was mere backdrop to the symphony erupting in her soul.

Peter lifted his head and his gaze met hers. His lips were full with lust, but his expression was vulnerable, the pupils of his eyes wide and black against a bed of emerald. She was suddenly afraid, knowing they should stop, knowing also that they wouldn't. She could not endure making love to Peter and finding herself frozen like ice to the past.

Then slowly, surely, Peter covered her mouth with his. The flame lighting her nerve endings erupted into a bonfire. His hands swept her back, over the curve of her buttocks and along her thighs. Heat spread like a tropical wind, streaking her skin until she raged out of control. She loosened her legs' grip and slid down his front, gasping when his hardness met her belly.

He tugged off her bathing suit bottom and she floated in the water before him, completely naked at last. Strangely, she felt no shyness, only urgency and need. She reached for him, her breathing rapid, and pulled off his trunks.

Nothing stood between them now. There seemed no wrong-doing, only an incredible rightness, an irrefutable lightness.

Floating towards him slowly, his body blazing hers with heat, she wrapped her arms around his neck. Then locking her legs around his hips, she settled snugly against him.

When he entered, she cried out, her anticipation of his touch paling at its reality, his long firm strokes filling and inflaming her with desire.

She clung to him, her fingers digging into his back, his thrusts soaring her to the pinnacle of sensation then down the other side, only to be shot aloft again on the roller coaster ride of passion.

The sun's warmth became lost in a maze of hot skin on hot skin, hardness piercing softness, wetness within and without, and everywhere . . . fire.

Flesh burning, nerves singing, their bodies played an exultation to the sacred Gods of the Islands. Their spirits soared together, their passion building to an impossible crescendo. Finally, in a volcanic explosion of heat, they vibrated against each other, involuntarily . . . lovingly.

Yet at the end, there was silence.

A silence so complete, Jann could hear Peter's heart pounding against her ear and the soundless lap of the water touching the shore, could hear the trill of the grasshoppers rubbing their legs together.

And beyond that silence came fear, as loud as the screech of a siren, and as jolting as the peel of an alarm. She buried her face against Peter's chest, desperate to still the noise, desperate, also, to hold on to what they had shared.

He held her now as though they had never been separated, as though he never intended to let her go again. But how could she stay?

She now knew the joy, the exhilarating ecstasy of truly making love, but in the making of love, she had realized she did love and the only possible finish to that was pain.

Pushing hard against Peter's chest, Jann fell backward through the icy water. She rose spluttering to find him reaching for her, and resolutely paddled beyond his grasp.

"We have to talk," he called after her, his voice low and insistent.

There was nothing to say. Only that they had made love and everything had changed. She could no longer trust herself to be near him, could not trust herself to do what was right.

He stroked powerfully through the water after her, and just as determinedly, she stroked away. If he touched her, she'd be lost. Sucking in a faltering breath, not caring about her bathing suit or if she retrieved it, she staggered up the rocky edge of the pond, resolved not to allow his magic to engulf her again.

The risk was too great. If she gave up her heart, it might be smashed under the heel of this stranger.

And she was not about to lose her baby because she couldn't hang on to her heart.

Snatching up her clothes, she flung them on. Peter emerged naked from the water, looking just as powerful as he had before and infinitely desirable. Her breath snagged as he moved toward her, the touch of his hand on her arm making her tremble.

"Why are you running?" he demanded, his eyes on fire.

She stood as tall as she was able, knowing with every fiber of her being that she loved this man, but knowing, too, that she could never let him know.

"We made a mistake." Her words created a void in her heart.

"Is that what you think?" He tilted up her chin, his eyes searching hers.

She ran her tongue over lips gone suddenly dry, her brain shying away from the knowledge of her love. She couldn't think about that now, not with him so close. He confused her, made her long for a life she couldn't have, for a love she dare not risk. To think rationally, with her head not her heart, she had to be alone.

Or she'd be lost. And if she was lost, so was Alex. "I'm not denying I enjoyed making love to you," she said, facing Peter squarely. Had reveled in it. "But it wasn't important." Simply life and death.

He gripped her arm so hard it hurt.

As she had that other time, she managed to laugh. She was getting good at this denial. If it went on much longer, it would be her soul that was destroyed.

"Men and women make love all the time without it having to mean anything," she went on, desperate to obliterate the pain in her heart.

He recoiled as though he'd been slapped.

Her breathing quickened.

He gave her a long hard look, his face whitening beneath his tan, then, with a slow intake of breath, he turned away. With all the will she possessed, she prevented words of retraction from escaping her lips.

This man was a stranger—not the man who had held her and listened to her and dispersed her guilt like dust in the wind. This man, clothed in the same expensive suit he'd worn the first day they met, was so distant, it was as if all that had gone between them had been a mirage.

And it hurt, though she had no one to blame but herself.

Shivering, Jann drew her forefinger across her lips, still craving his touch. Somehow, impossibly, she had summoned the strength to deny that craving.

At the pool's edge, Peter had turned from her and slowly dressed. It had been terrible to watch the way he held himself, the way his muscles tightened across his shoulders and his neck corded with strain. Almost . . . almost as though he truly cared.

A drop of sweat dripped slowly down Jann's hairline. She longed to wipe it away, to be rid of the evidence of her distress, but if she made any movement, if she pulled her hankie from her dress pocket, Peter would look at her again, and if he did that, another part of her would die.

She had fled from him once already. She couldn't bring herself to do it again. Before he had finished dressing, she had left the magic of the pool behind, plunging down the steep pathway until she reached the car. Flinging herself into it, she held herself stiffly against the door, averting her eyes from his and praying he would let her be.

And he had. Without a word or gesture, he climbed in beside her and started the engine. With blinding precision, he had driven the ocean highway back to Lahaina; while she sat frozen, determined not to show fear even when they passed the steepest cliff.

Now there was the dance to get through. She had told him she preferred to go alone, but when the time came to leave, he had settled into the rowboat with a stubborn cast to his lips. He walked beside her now as though he were in a race, his quick, angry steps shutting her out more effectively than she had him.

Music poured from the hall and bathed the town in sound. She tried to close her ears to it, to keep its beat at bay, for she loved to dance, had spent hours when she was young watching her parents pirouette around the living room locked in each other's embrace. Sometimes separately, sometimes together, her mother and father had taught her the steps to every dance they knew, until, exhausted, they had all collapsed together on the sofa, helpless with happiness and laughter.

But she didn't want to dance tonight. Not with Peter. Holding herself apart from him was as difficult as withdrawing from a drug. If she fell into his arms, she might never come out.

For rightly or wrongly, she loved him.

Jann lifted her chin. If she could get through tonight, that left only tomorrow. Then, she'd be safe. She'd be home. With Alex.

First thing Monday morning, she would phone Mitch. It would be better now if Peter did have unsupervised access, for she could no longer be near him and not betray how she felt.

Glancing sideways, she squashed the last pang of her old apprehension. She knew enough about Peter now to know he would never steal her baby. He might be ruthless and determined, but it wasn't his style to slink away in the dark of the night. His personal code of honor was too scrupulous for that.

He turned to look at her. "Planning on running away again?" he asked, his words hard, though his voice was even.

She gazed at him squarely, though her insides turned to water. The pulse at the base of his throat throbbed and he lifted his hand as though he couldn't stop himself from touching her. At the last possible instant, he let his hand drop.

The music's volume suddenly surged.

"Something happened at the Pools," Peter said. "Running won't make it go away."

"I'm not running away."

He drew closer. "We need to talk."

"No," she said quietly, yet with a vehemence that shook her. "Talking won't change anything."

"You don't know that."

"The only thing between you and me is Alex. He's all we should be concerning ourselves with."

She turned and rapidly walked away, but he followed her up the short flight of stairs to the hall. In the doorway she faced him again, meeting his questioning eyes.

"We have to stay away from each other," she said firmly.

"How do you suggest we do that on a forty-foot sailboat in the middle of an ocean?"

"It's thirty-seven feet," she corrected, then nodded toward the crowd on the dance floor. "And at the moment, we're not in the middle of an ocean."

"You're right." His gaze shifted to the mass of gyrating merry-makers, then came back to her. "But what if I don't choose to stay away from you." He took a step closer.

His words settled coldly in the pit of her stomach. Then with a suddenness that stole her breath, he reached for her camera bag and handed it to the coat check girl. Gathering Jann's hand in his, he placed his other hand on the small of her back, and swept her away.

The race was over and the party had begun. Triumphant hands waved champagne bottles high and corks popped like bullets in a battle. Glasses were filled, spilled, and filled once more. Throughout the room, caution was flung to the winds and a bubbly effervescence took its place.

The dance floor was a mine field of swirling, sweaty bodies and over-enthusiastic contortions. Holding tightly to her waist, Peter steered Jann into the middle of the melee.

Within minutes she was breathless. Peter danced the way he moved—with precision and grace. He swirled her and twirled her, her turquoise dress flying up one moment and streaking down the next.

The exuberant atmosphere gradually lifted Jann's mood, while at the same time deadened her apprehensions. Her heart felt less leaden, and her body took on a lightness.

Then as the band belted out the final bars of an old sixties rock and roll song, a dancer bumped heavily into Jann, pushing her hard against Peter's chest.

The world seemed to stop.

His hand tightened on her waist and they swayed together as one, her breasts flattened against his chest and her hips thrust forward.

His eyes searched hers, reaching into her soul and demanding a response. Her heart quailed, knowing there was no way she could hide the love she felt for him, no way she could deny it.

The air grew still, like the deathly silence before a storm, and Jann staggered beneath the weight of a surging desire.

Then the band started afresh, sliding into a sensuous pulsation of heart-wrenching blues. The music tore at her soul, biting through her defenses and opening her heart to the air.

Where they touched, there was heat; where they didn't, she was numb. Her hands stole up Peter's arms and linked at the base of his neck.

He touched her bare back where her dress dipped sharply, his spine-tingling caress electrifying her. With deliberate slowness, he pulled her closer.

Slower and slower, they danced. Hotter and hotter. Like lava over rock.

He laid his cheek against her cheek, his newly shaven skin smooth and warm. His scent was intoxicating, its blend of musk and vibrant sea breezes filling Jann's nostrils and weakening her with desire.

Leaning away from him, she stared up into eyes turned a lustrous smoky-green. Solemnly, searchingly, Peter lowered his head and kissed her.

His mouth moved slowly over hers at first, as though reluctant to release any portion of her lips to the air, then with greater intensity, matching the cadence of the song. Note fell upon note, kiss deepened into kiss, until Jann neither knew nor cared where Peter's lips left off and her own began.

Sensation erupted within, beginning with a tremor and mounting swiftly into a crescendo. Helpless with desire and shaken to the core, she sank against him.

Then, as suddenly as it had begun, the song ended. With a roaring in Jann's ears, her blood flooded through her veins and the sound of Peter's heart beat into her consciousness. She clung to him as tightly as a ship-wrecked sailor to a beam.

Another song began, but although other dancers boogied, the two of them barely moved. Like two boats rafted together awaiting rescue in a storm, they were buffeted to and fro by the music surrounding them.

Peter's hand drifted up Jann's back and trailed along her neck to her chin. He gently tipped her face upward, his eyes locking with hers. She could see in them how he felt as clearly as if he had spoken.

He wanted to make love to her again, and was fighting that want.

Raising her hand to her crystal, she examined her own soul. She wasn't sure whether it was the crystal pulsing beneath her hand or simply the rapid thumping of her heart, but suddenly she knew with all her heart, mind, and body, that she wanted to make love to Peter as much as he did to her. That she would rather drown in his arms than catch a lifeboat to safety.

"Let's go," Peter growled.

"Yes," Jann breathed, not moving an inch.

Placing his arm around her shoulders, Peter pulled her along with him, marking a path through the dancers as easily as a ship with radar. People jostled and flailed against her, but

Jann scarcely noticed. She could think only of Peter and the way he made her feel.

Through the hall's smoky haze, the sharp outline of the open door was visible. The brilliant stars beyond transmitted a promise of passion so powerful, Jann trembled.

Peter pulled her closer, the warm haven of his body stilling her shivers.

She could no longer hide how she felt, no longer wanted to. Her longing must be as evident in her eyes as in the flushed heat of her face.

Barely slowing as they passed the cloakroom, Peter retrieved Jann's cameras and led her out the door.

Away from the building, the night's breeze was as soft as the breath of a baby. Touched by the cool of the evening air, the flowers lining the streets and wafting overhead in baskets, trees, and bushes threw off a fairyland mixture of intoxicating fragrances.

Nearer the docks, the scent became that of salt and sea breezes, lodging in Jann's heart as a symbol of taking chances.

Her heels tapped softly on the rickety wooden boards of the dock as they made their way toward the rowboat. Once in it, his oars sliding smoothly through the water, Peter propelled them towards *HEART'S DESIRE* like two love birds flying homeward to their roost.

Jann raised her hand to her face, grateful now for the cover of darkness. The desire she felt for Peter had erupted on her cheeks in two feverish patches. Panic, too, bubbled in her chest. When they had first met, Peter had suggested he believed her well experienced in the art of making love. At the pools, too, their lovemaking had been spontaneous and fever-lit. On her boat, with privacy and time, would he expect something she couldn't deliver? Would she give him her all and have nothing left?

The rowboat bumped gently against her sailboat's hull.

Grasping the metal rung of the ladder, Jann slipped off her high heels and flung them into the cockpit, then climbed the ladder in her bare feet, piercingly aware of Peter as he followed slowly behind.

Scrambling over the side, she welcomed the warmth of the teak deck beneath her toes. Peter dropped down beside her and touched the curve of her waist. She faced him.

# Chapter Thirteen

Peter's eyes smoldered like emeralds in a chest of king's ransom. Then he draped his arms across her shoulders and pulled her trembling body close.

As soon as they touched, a trembling of another, more intimate sort welled within. She eagerly offered him her lips.

Desire transformed the lines of his face, softening them with want and rendering them vulnerable. He dropped one tender kiss on the corner of her mouth then ranged up her cheek and across her forehead, burning a pattern of love on her skin. Passion rose, and she met his sensuality with her own.

As weightless as the touch of the butterfly, as intoxicating as a drink of cognac, Peter's lips alighted on hers. Softly, at first, then hardening into urgency, he kissed . . . then withdrew . . . then kissed again.

Heat raced through Jann's veins, her nipples hardening and her breasts filling. She needed to be touched, to be captured by his lips. With a soft moan, she pressed against him, bathing in the sensations continuously washing over her.

She spiraled upward on a wave of desire, then just when it seemed she could go no higher, his lips deserted hers and traveled slowly . . . deliriously slowly . . . down her throat toward her breasts.

He cupped them with his hands so they rose from the confines of her scoop-necked dress and glistened in the light of the moon.

"I want you," he murmured against her throat. "I need you." He pulled her towards him as though he would never let her go, then, with a suddenness that seemed to stun, for his face stared starkly into hers, he drew away.

As slowly as he'd retreated, her heart broke.

"Peter," she whispered, reaching for him, touching his face with her finger.

Laboriously, slowly, he drew in a breath, as though the mere act of breathing was beyond his capabilities.

"You're so beautiful," he said hoarsely, then glancing to the sky above, his lips turned down in a rueful smile. "More beautiful than the stars."

Shocked by the desire exploding within and the numbness following in its wake, she stared past his eyes and up toward the heavens, amazed at the comparison he had made. A meteor blazed overhead, its passage piercing the night's blackness as her love for Peter pierced her soul.

"Peter," she whispered, surrender in her heart.

He stared down at her, and she felt his body go rigid.

"Jann . . ." He turned away. ". . .we can't do this. We have to talk about Alex."

Despair and fear rocketed through her. She'd fallen in love with Peter, had dared to think he might love her too, but their love was as unattainable as the stars, as impossible.

On unsteady feet, she turned away and staggered down the companionway to her cabin.

Jann clung to her coffee mug with both hands and lowered her face to the steam rising from the hot, black liquid. If only the steam could obliterate what she was feeling, could cover it in a cloak of opaque whiteness and dull the pain. With a sigh, she scanned the sky. It overflowed still with stars, each more brilliant than the lights on a Christmas tree, but each star seemed a lie, for there was no illumination in her heart.

Peter was back on board at last, was sleeping below deck. She had heard him leave as she retreated, had heard the scrape of his shoes against the ladder and the splash of his oars as they hit the water. A sound that had grown softer as the rowboat drew away. As each stroke increased the distance between them, Jann's heart had broken a little more.

It had seemed then as though she had sat on the edge of her bed for hours, though according to the snail-slow hands of her clock, it was only a fraction of that time.

And then he was back, his footsteps quick and determined, as though he felt nothing of the anguish engulfing her. The creak of the settee told her just when he lay down.

Her loins ached to think of him asleep, with his face more vulnerable than wakefulness would allow. For she still wanted him, and in a way not merely physical. She wanted his body and also his soul, but most of all she desired his heart.

A lump blocked her throat. Though they had made love at the Pools, his heart was not hers. The passion they had shared had been nothing more than the insistent pulsation of blood, the magic of the rainbow, and the physical need between two people.

Peter obviously wanted to forget it, was regretting their lovemaking as a tactical error in his quest for Alex.

She cringed with shame to think she'd mistaken it for so much more. If she'd stuck to what she'd known, that to fall in love was to be unsafe, she wouldn't be feeling now the pain she was enduring.

When she made love to Peter, she had broken her cardinal rule. To undo the damage, she had to return to her normal life, had to get back to Alex and feel safe once more. If she could hold her baby in her arms, she might be able to collect her bearings, might not be blinded by passion and the heat of desire.

Acting swiftly, so as not to change her mind, Jann scrambled down the stairs into the chart room and turned the key in the ignition.

The sudden growl of the engine shattered the peace of the tropical night like the revving of a motor cycle might do at a symphony. Hurrying back up the steps, Jann hauled the anchor from the water and steered the boat toward open sea.

She couldn't see Peter, but she heard the thump of his feet when he rolled off the settee and pounded up the companionway.

Her heart was pounding, too, by the time he appeared, pulling on his trousers, but carrying his shirt. In the moonlight, his tanned chest glowed like warm sand.

Desire arrowed through her, swift and unexpected. Catching her lower lip between her teeth, she tried to will it away.

"What the hell do you think you're doing?" He swept sleep-tousled hair back from his eyes.

"Going home," she replied firmly, determined not to cry. But when she stared into his eyes, she was unable to keep the tears from spilling.

"I need to see Alex," she added, brushing the moisture away. Not the whole truth, but close enough.

"You're running away," he accused, his eyes bleak and angry. Shrugging into his shirt, he stepped toward her, the tangy scent of his aftershave making her long to touch him.

"Why not?" she flung back. "You did." Clenching her lips, she tightened her grip on the wheel.

His jaw tightened, and he stumbled, as if from the force of the truth she spoke. "Maybe you're right," he said quietly. "Maybe it's time we faced what we're feeling."

"No!" she cried, her stomach knotting at the idea.

"You're afraid," he accused, as he'd accused once before.

"Yes!" she admitted, then followed it with, "No!" She shut her eyes, not knowing how she felt, knowing only that she wanted him with an intensity that burned, also knowing that if she had him, her pain would only worsen. She could scarcely bear the silence that met her words.

"You can't steer with your eyes shut," he said at last, seeming to strive for lightness, but nowhere in his voice, could she detect laughter.

He touched her shoulder, and her soul was touched, too, his warmth and strength irresistible, his appeal as strong as before. She jerked away, opened her eyes, and with a deep breath turned to face him.

"Where did you go?" she demanded.

"To shore," he replied. "I needed to be alone."

Her heart was breaking and he needed solitude!

He put his hand on the wheel. "I'll take over here," he said. "Make us some coffee, then we'll talk."

Her legs seemed incapable of movement.

He glanced out at the water, then slowly turned his gaze back to her. "If you really want to go home, we will, but first we need to talk."

She no longer had a home. Home was where Peter was, and she couldn't have that.

For he hadn't said he loved her.

He hadn't said anything at all.

Except that she was more beautiful than the stars.

Easy to say.

Sucking in a breath, she forced her feet toward the companionway. Once down in the galley, she grimly poured coffee into two cups and set the cups on a tray. The coffee was too thick and too black, but it was the best she could do.

On leaden feet, she trudged back up the stairs, longing, instead, to bury herself in her bunk and pull the covers over her head. But even there, no doubt, she'd be besieged by images of Peter and the joy she had felt when they made love.

Steeling herself, she stepped out into the cockpit and handed Peter his cup. Lahaina was already receding into the distance, the lights of the harbor glowing like fireflies beyond their stern.

"What time is it?" Peter asked, gulping down a mouthful of the hot liquid.

"Almost midnight," she replied, peering at her watch.

"We should make Honolulu by eight o'clock," he said tonelessly.

Eight long hours and it would be over. She bit her lip. Never over, no matter how many hours it was.

"What's the weather forecast?" he asked, glancing up at the sky.

"I didn't check it."

"You didn't check it?" he demanded, his voice incredulous.

"No, I . . . I just decided to leave."

Disbelief filled his eyes.

"I'll check it now." Ducking through the hatch, she moved down to the chart room and went straight for the marine radio.

It wasn't on.

Cold water dashing over her couldn't have shocked her more. She had turned the radio off this morning before they left the boat, but she hadn't turned it back on again, hadn't listened at the scheduled air time for possible messages, or phoned Ruby today, either.

What if Ruby and John had been trying to contact her? Had needed her?

She swallowed hard, tried to convince herself there was little likelihood of either of those things happening.

Flicking the radio switch to the 'On' position, Jann pushed the weather channel button down. The reassuring voice of the announcer proclaimed a twenty knot wind in the channel.

Relieved, she increased the volume and turned the knob to the marine band. Static, interspersed with messages to mariners, crackled from the receiver. She listened for a moment, then turned up the volume loud enough to be heard on deck.

"Well?" Peter asked, his gaze flickering towards her as she emerged through the hatch.

"The trades are blowing in the channel, but nothing to worry about."

"Never underestimate the weather," he said, making an infinitesimal adjustment of the wheel to starboard.

"I—"

"*HEART'S DESIRE. HEART'S DESIRE.* This is *WIND-WARD.* Are you there? Come in, come in." The message squealing from the receiver faded in and out as though the volume knob was being spun by an over-excited two-year-old.

Alarm slid like ice into Jann's chest. "Alex," she whispered, her body frozen numb.

"You don't know that," Peter countered, his hands flying as he set up the self-steering. "Answer them!" he urged.

She scrambled down the steps. Peter slipped out from behind the wheel and followed swiftly after her. She came to a halt in front of the radio, immobilized, terrified.

"Answer it," he repeated, more gently this time.

Fear filled her heart.

"It'll be all right." His gaze held hers. Strong eyes, reassuring.

Clenching her jaw, Jann picked up the mike. "This is *HEART'S DESIRE*," she said, then said it again more firmly. "*HEART'S DESIRE* here. Over."

"Dammit, girl, is that you? We've been trying to reach you all day. Over."

All day? John and Ruby had been trying to reach her while she had been lost in lovemaking?

"Jann here, Capt'n," she identified, her voice sounding faint although the cabin was small. "What's the problem?" She could only pray that whatever it was, it had nothing to do with Alex. "Over."

She caught her breath while she waited for Capt'n's response, wishing Peter would hold her.

"It's Alex." John said, his voice sounding older and shakier than she remembered.

Her shoulders stiffened. Peter moved closer and put his arm around her waist.

"He's in . . . pital. Over." The radio screeched as static took over all other sound.

"He's where? Over."

"In hospital. Dammit girl. Ain't you listening? Over."

Her hands began to tremble, her hold on the mike loosening. Peter snatched the instrument from her.

"Peter Strickland here. What's the matter with Alexander? Over."

"Gastroenteritis." The medical term wavered with the vagaries of the machine in front of them. "The poor little mite's wasting away to nothing." Now it was John's voice that quavered, not the machine into which he spoke.

Jann sat down hard onto a chair, a roaring filling her ears. Peter's lips were moving but she could hear no sound. After what seemed an eternity, he signed off, and placed the mike on the table.

He looked at her, his eyes soft with concern. The caring in his face somehow gave her some strength and the roaring in her ears dulled to a buzz.

"We'll head back to Maui and fly to Oahu," Peter said crisply.

"At this hour?" Jann cried. "There'll be no planes until morning."

"There'll be a plane." His eyes grew hard with determination. "I'll hire one."

She couldn't speak through a throat that felt like grating sandpaper. She could only nod, grateful that Peter was there making the decisions.

"We'll be with Alexander soon," he added, gently touching her arm.

"It doesn't sound good," she whispered. "Vomiting,

diarrhea. Baby's can die when they get dehydrated." She stared hard into Peter's eyes. "He's so little."

"They've got him hooked up to an IV. That'll control the dehydration."

"I never should have left him."

Peter came closer still, and reaching out his hand, gently stroked her hair. His touch soothed.

If only the cabin hadn't turned to ice. If only she weren't so cold.

Peter ceased his caress and held out his hand for her to hold. For a long moment, she simply stared at it, her tears frozen in her eyes. Then she looked into his eyes and found them darker than midnight. His unsmiling lips were pinched white around the edges. But his hand, when she took it, was as hot as an electric blanket.

"Alex will be all right," he said huskily, pulling her to her feet and drawing her into his arms.

His touch warmed her on the surface, but inside, she still froze. From between open lips, her breath escaped shallowly. Peter's shirt lay comfortingly soft against her cheek.

"Alex's illness must have been coming on when we left," she said haltingly, her heart contracting with self-loathing. "He was fussing, was hot." She took a deep breath. "Ruby said it was teething."

She pushed Peter away, stared bleakly into his eyes. "I never should have left him," she repeated dully.

# Chapter Fourteen

The face staring back at her from the door's much-polished glass couldn't possibly be hers. She looked like a madwoman. Her strawberry blonde curls swirled around her head in a fashion impenetrable by any comb, and her eyes were blue-black saucers much too large for her face.

Peter yanked open the door to the children's ward and Jann sidled past, trying not to touch him, for if she did, the wall she'd so painstakingly built around herself would crack and she'd fly into his arms and beg to stay there forever.

Peter didn't need that. He looked no better than she. His skin was as pale as marble against his rumpled black hair and his mouth was set in a grim line. He'd said little when she'd claimed responsibility for Alex's condition, perhaps knowing there was nothing he could say to make her feel better, to lift the burden of blame from her shoulders.

Jerking her gaze from Peter, she stared down the long corridor. She had been in a frenzy to get here, desperate to see Alex with her own eyes, needing to hold him. But now they had arrived, she could scarcely bear to go on, hating that she couldn't alleviate her baby's suffering, terrified she would doom him with her presence.

Thrusting her shoulders straight, she forced one foot in front of the other, the only way she could make it any closer to Alex. She was excruciatingly aware of Peter at her side, not needing to touch him or see him to know that he was there. Needle-thin cords seemed to stretch between them, connecting them, binding them, one to the other.

The lights on the ceiling were unbearably bright, the floor, with its squares within squares, dizzying. Opening her eyes wide, she bit hard on her lip, but the pattern on the linoleum continued to swirl, and along with it, her mind.

Then Peter caught her hand and the dizziness disappeared, leaving only the terrified pounding of her heart. Everything frightened her lately. It didn't used to be so. Not before Alex. Not before Peter.

CHILDREN'S INTENSIVE CARE.

The words might have been written in neon the way they stood out. Jann's pounding heart slowed. Or maybe it was her breathing that slowed, for she couldn't find enough air.

Peter gave her hand a squeeze, then releasing it, put his arm around her waist. She sank against him, needing him too much to resist him now, needing the strength only he could give her. Pushing open the door to the ward, he guided her through in front of him.

Room 326. She couldn't see the number. Was it down another corridor? No. The even numbers were on the right like house numbers on a street. Laughter bubbled up, threatening to escape. She clamped her lips shut, pushing the hysteria away.

Alex needed her.

This was not her parents' room.

Nor Claire's.

Alex was not about to die!

Room 326. At last.

She took a deep breath, mustering her courage to open the door, but before she could do so, Peter pulled her into his arms. His heart beat savagely against her ear, but his arms were rock solid.

Like the man himself.

For a single, blissful moment Jann felt completely safe.

He tilted her face upward, and though he made no move to kiss her, power rocketed through her, lending her courage. When they had made love, it had been magic, today his touch held strength. Looking deep into his eyes, she found the courage to go on.

She opened the door. There were too many patients, too many visitors. The space was bursting with noise and confusion.

Except for Alex, who lay silent.

His body was too tiny for such a big bed, his gurgles and cries stilled. Covered in a sheen of perspiration, he seemed to have shrunk during the three days she'd been gone. His face was gaunt and his precious baby fat had all but disappeared, leaving only loose skin wrinkling around skinny legs.

Except for his diaper, her baby was naked. His quilt lay on top of him. The one she had made. Under a panoply of stars, the porpoise still danced on the end of its tail.

Incongruous somehow, with Alex so sick.

Tears stung Jann's eyes. She'd made him that quilt after Claire died, as a promise to Claire's child that she'd always do her best.

Somehow she had failed.

Ruby rose stiffly from the chair beside Alex's bed. "Thank goodness you're here," she whispered as Jann hurried forward. The old woman gave Jann a hug. "Alex has been wanting you. I'm so sorry, Jann. I was sure he was simply teething."

Jann wrenched her gaze from her child and turned to her friend, heartsick at the sight of tears in the older woman's eyes.

"It's not your fault, Ruby," she whispered. "It's mine."

She dragged a chair next to Alex's bed and wearily sat down. Her baby lay so still. Only his eyelids fluttered as he slept and his chest rose, then fell again, with the release of a shallow breath.

His intravenous stood next to his bed, so big, so adult a machine for such a little guy. When Jann lifted Alex's hand, she found his fingers as waxy and lifeless as a doll's. She massaged them gently, willing them to warm and turn their familiar pink.

Peter wedged himself in on the other side of the bed, his

brows drawn together and his lips a grim slash.

"What's he doing in a room like this?" he demanded.

"I don't know," Jann said helplessly, then glanced toward Ruby.

"It was all your medical insurance would cover," Ruby explained softly.

Peter's face grew more thunderous.

Even that small insurance had been more than she could afford. The pulse at Jann's temple pounded in unison with the bleep of the monitor at the head of Alex's bed.

A nurse entered the room carrying a tray laden with pills. Peter called her over with a jerk of his arm.

"I want this child in a private room," he said, "with a private nurse."

He was giving orders again, Jann thought dazedly, but she welcomed it this time as she had the night before. She could only pray his efforts would make a difference.

Back on Maui, she had phoned the hospital while Peter arranged for the plane. Alex's doctor hadn't been able to tell her what had caused the baby's gastroenteritis, but had indicated it could have been any number of things. A bacteria. A virus. A tropical germ. His environment.

By the time she and Peter had arrived in Honolulu, the culprit had been found. The supply of water on her boat was to blame, water stored in an aging holding tank, pumped up through old pipes and dribbled out through leaking faucets. She'd put off the repairs many times, thinking she couldn't afford them, but it looked now as though they might cost her everything she held dear.

Over the telephone, the doctor had sounded reassuring, but when they saw that same doctor at the front desk on the way in, his eyes had held worry. Jann knew the dangers of dehydration in a child as young as Alex, but tried hard to cling to the doctor's initial certainty, to trust in that opinion. To do that she had to eliminate the memory of her parents' death, and of Claire's death, too.

Fear, as sharp-edged as a diamond, lodged in her throat. She tried to swallow, but managed only a strangled gurgle. Peter cast her a swift glance, then took hold of Alex's other hand, caressing the baby's skin with a slow sweep of his thumb.

She had witnessed Peter's gentleness before, when he held Alex or changed his diapers, when he'd made the baby giggle in a rousing game of peek-a-boo, but she hadn't allowed herself to value that gentleness, hadn't dared to even acknowledge it. Now it loomed before her, as damning as her guilt.

Alex pulled his legs to his chest and emitted a shallow mew. His eyes opened for an instant, then fluttered shut once more. Peter stroked Alex's tummy in a circular motion, seeming to know instinctively where it hurt and how to fix it. Fixing what she had broken. What she was responsible for.

Pressing shaking fingers against her brow, Jann prayed the pressure would take away the pain, feeling idiotically hopeful that because she was suffering, Alex's suffering might disappear.

Ruby touched her shoulder, saying she and John were going home. They were worn out, Jann realized sickly, by the vigil they had kept. A vigil she should have been here to keep herself.

The day passed in a blur and ended in a fog, the muted ceiling lamp the only indication night had fallen, and the chinks of light showing around the edges of the curtains the only sign dawn was upon them again. A stiffness pervaded Jann's body, forbidding movement. Numbness infiltrated her brain, stifling all thought.

The only clarity was the hands clasped on the white sheet in front of her, Alex's hand in Peter's and Alex's hand in her own. She longed to take hold of Peter's other hand and complete the circle of hearts and bodies, for that seemed the only way her baby would get better. But to reach for Peter seemed as impossible now as reaching for the stars.

She touched her crystal instead, its smooth surface strangely cold and unresponsive. When she slipped it from around her neck and held it in her open hand, its color disappeared along with its warmth, its usual translucent pink chillingly subdued.

The crystal, with its shafts of light and splashes of reflected color, had always fascinated Alex. He would reach for it, squealing with delight, and with plump fingers pat at it as though it were alive.

With a swift glance at her baby's pale face, Jann tucked the crystal into his hand and pressed his fingers shut around it. She wasn't sure what she expected to happen, but it wasn't this nothingness of expression, this paucity of reaction. Even when she took his hand in hers, Alex didn't move.

Heartsick, she stared across Alex's inert form and looked at Peter instead. For the past eighteen hours, she had focused only on her baby, convinced that unless she did so some irreversible harm would occur. But she needed Peter's strength, as a yawning hole needs filling, as grass needs rain, and flowers sunshine.

Yet she couldn't acknowledge that need, couldn't allow it to even exist. For if she did, she'd be vulnerable, and she had promised herself never to be vulnerable again. She had attempted throughout the night to expunge all images of Peter from her brain: his lips, the safety of his arms, his eyes . . . especially his eyes, with their ability to see into hers and know, as only a soul mate would know, what she was thinking and what she was feeling.

But she had failed in her efforts. He lingered in her mind as he did on the periphery of her vision, warming her to her heart's core and her soul's center. Impossible to block. Impossible to ignore.

His strength was her strength, his warmth hers also. The first time Alex cried out so feebly in the night, she froze, turned to Peter and, for an instant, long enough for her to grip more tightly to her courage, the ice retreated and her soul readied itself to meet the new horrors ahead.

Then Peter stared at her without smiling, his lips seeming blue in the unearthly morning light and his skin as white as the hospital walls. His eyes were filled with pain, but even thus didn't waver.

Her heart felt as brittle as ice across a puddle. A little more pressure and everything would shatter.

Without speaking, without seeming to move, Peter took her hand in his. A circle of hands now lay on the sheet, strong in its beginning and strong again at its end, a circle linking them as a family was linked, as a circle of light capable of piercing the darkness.

Heat, fiery as lava and faster than lightning, traveled from Peter's hand to hers, then along her arm to her body and from there to her heart. Alex stirred as though he felt it too, his eyes fluttering open and focusing on Jann's face, the faintest of sounds whispering from between his dry lips. Enclosed in her hand, Alex's fingers tightened around the crystal.

Even his body seemed different now. Maybe it was his color, with the suggestion of pink dusting his pale cheeks, or maybe it was the small movement.

Whatever the difference, as Jann stared across at Peter her heart filled with gratitude.

And with love.

She straightened, new strength filling her with hope. She did love Peter. Needed him. Trusted him.

When had it happened? This trust.

This knowledge that Peter loved Alex.

As much as she did.

Was as good a parent as she.

Probably better.

The knot of fear lodged in her throat expanded to overrun her heart. She mustn't think of what a good parent Peter would make. Had to think of the future instead. Plan for when Alex got out of this place.

She drew herself up. Living on the boat had done this thing to Alex. Peter had been right when he said a boat was no place for a baby.

Her heart ached in protest, but she couldn't stop her thoughts.

Alex would be better off with Peter in his ancestral home, even with Claire's old nanny to help care for him. Claire's nanny might not be the aloof, clinical woman the matron of her orphanage had been. She might be warm, might love Alex as a proper nanny should. And Alex would have Peter as a father, a blood relative, one who could give him everything he needed. Including love.

Especially love.

She hadn't allowed herself to see it before. Much easier to cling to the wishes Claire had made so clear.

But Claire had been wrong. Young, angry and alone, she hadn't realized how much Peter loved her, how desperately he had tried to keep her safe. He had got it wrong at times, but not for lack of caring.

The tears started unexpectedly, racing unchecked down Jann's cheeks. She couldn't seem to make them stop, even when she blindly squeezed Alex's hand, holding it so tightly the crystal dropped from his fingers. She picked it up again, needing the strength it gave her to do what she had to do, not sure even then if she had the courage.

Raising her other hand to her baby's face, she traced the outline of his delicate features with her fingertips. If she concentrated hard enough, his image would be imprinted on her soul forever. As would Peter's.

If she truly loved Alex, she would find the courage to do what was right, would sacrifice her own needs for his, as mothers had been doing since the beginning of time.

As the mother who had appeared before King Solomon had done. When two women both claimed a baby as their own, the King had commanded the baby be divided into two. The true mother hadn't allowed that, had given her baby to the other woman rather than see him hurt.

As Jann would give.

Alex would be better off with Peter. If she loved her child enough, she must find the courage to let him go.

With a long shuddering sob, she pulled her hand from Alex's face and stared at Peter through tear-blurred eyes.

"He's yours," she whispered, not looking at Alex as she spoke, for if she looked at him, she might not do what she knew was right.

"What do you mean?" Peter asked, his emerald eyes darkening to a velvety blackness.

"You want him," she said, struggling to keep her voice audible. "You can have him." Then she turned away, her eyes awash with tears, loving Peter as thoroughly, as gut-wrenchingly as she loved Alex. By giving one to the other, she'd lose them both.

But they'd also both be safe and that was all that mattered.

Lowering her head, she pressed Alex's hand to her lips. For the space of a kiss, she held it there, then gently dropped it back to the sheet.

Allowing herself one last glance at Peter—any more would be fatal to her resolve—she stood. Her heart shattering, she strangled back a cry and raced for the door.

When it swung shut behind her, she slumped against the wall, tears coursing down her cheeks and her breath coming in hard gasps. Etched into her brain was the sight of Peter's face; his skin white, his eyes black with disbelief.

Peter . . . . She pressed her eyes closed.

A rush of air crossed her face. She felt, rather than saw, the door beside her open. A strong hand gripped her arm.

"You're giving him to me?"

Opening her eyes, she found Peter standing before her, his green gaze burning hers. She nodded, unable to trust her voice.

"Just like that?" he demanded hoarsely.

She nodded again, trembling.

"So when the going gets rough, you bail out." The fury in his eyes was mixed with contempt.

There seemed not enough air to fill her lungs. Jann leaned over, her hands on her knees. One breath. Two. The sick feeling abated and the wild pounding of her heart steadied to a dull roar. She slowly straightened.

"If it helps you to think that, then believe it," she whispered. Tiny arrows of pain seemed to pierce her from all directions. After all she and Peter had shared, how could he believe that was why she was giving him her son?

"What else can I think?"

If he had shouted, she could have stood it better. This coldness was worse than anything.

"Tell me," he demanded, his fingers tightening around her wrist.

"You'll make a good father," she said.

He clamped his other hand on her shoulder.

"Let go of me." She shrugged his hand away. She couldn't do this if he touched her.

He drew back as though he had been burned, but she could feel the heat where his fingers had lain. Glancing at her shoulder, she half expected to find the outline of his palm burned into her skin.

"I've seen you with Alex," Peter said, his voice low and furious.

Holding him, loving him. Jann's eyes stung with tears.

"You're a good mother."

She stared up at him, stunned. "Not good enough," she said, choking. Though, the Lord knew she had tried. But in the end, she had failed. Peter wouldn't fail.

"You love him."

"I left him when he was sick."

"You didn't know."

"I should have known."

"This isn't just about Alex." Peter reached for her again. "It's about you and me, too."

"No," she said fiercely, the pain in her chest threatening to obliterate the pain in her head.

If he didn't love her, how could this be about the two of them? And he'd never said he did love her. Not yesterday. Not now.

Jann closed her eyes, shutting out the light and shutting out Peter.

Let him go.

If she loved him, she had to let him go.

She forced her eyes open. Miraculously, her body had ceased its trembling. The palms of her hands were dry when she pressed her fingers into them.

"When he's better, I'll take him to the boat until you're ready to leave. But after that," she said flatly, turning on her heel, "Alex is yours." She followed the line of the linoleum, weaving as though she were drunk, but no matter how much she wavered, she didn't look back.

# Chapter Fifteen

Alex's left hand latched onto Jann's hair, and he pulled her head down, giggling as she buried her face in his tummy. It was all she could do to keep from crying, but there'd been too much of that lately, especially at night, and in the shower. Wherever no one could hear.

Alex was better, though it had taken over a week. A little thinner, a little quieter, but his old self nonetheless now he was back in his own home. At least now when she gave him away, she'd know he wasn't going to have to face his new home feeling ill.

As she'd had to do. Was it the second or the third time she'd been moved? When her foster parents of the moment had decided their commitment didn't extend to wiping sweat-filled foreheads and sitting up half the night waiting for her fever to go down.

Jann tickled Alex's toes, tried to forget her long ago pain. She smiled back at him when he laughed, savoring the sound of his joy and locking it in her heart to be pulled out when he was no longer with her.

Peter would be here soon, as he had been every day in the week since Alex had returned home, though on those other days he had usually come in the evening, after hours filled with lawyers, courts and travel arrangements.

He seemed to want to avoid contact with Jann as much as she did with him, arriving only in time to kiss Alex good night, but holding himself apart from her, as though there had never been warmth between them, as though he had never touched her at all.

It hurt. As she had known that it would.

In just a few moments, he'd be here again, but in the cold light of morning this time, and he would take her baby from her, and himself, too.

Thrusting her face back into Alex's belly, she prayed hard that her baby's laughter would keep her tears at bay. She couldn't cry again. Not in front of Peter.

Then she heard it. The soft padding of shoes on wood. Even the slap of water against the boat's hull couldn't drown out the sound.

Peter was here.

It was too soon.

Panic filled her chest. Now that the time had come, could she actually do this thing she had promised? She stared down at Alex. For his sake, she had to.

She picked him up, held him close. He clutched her shirt with one hand while the other pumped the air.

John and Ruby stepped off their own boat as Peter passed, leaving their coffee mugs behind on the *WINDWARD'S* wooden deck. They stood together, faces solemn, arms around each others' waists.

"Is he ready?" Peter asked, looking only at her, not looking at Alex at all.

Alex was, she wasn't. She could only nod. She couldn't speak.

"He's packed?"

Couldn't he see Alex's bag lying on the dock beside him? Maybe by giving her questions to which she had only to nod, he was trying to make this easier for her. Maybe he knew that if she opened her mouth, she would beg him to ignore the offer she had made in the hospital, and rescinding that offer of custody was something he wasn't prepared to risk.

He suddenly stepped aboard, leaving Alex's bag where it lay. She had tucked the picture of Claire inside the bag, knowing that Peter liked it and wanting Alex to have that memento of his mother. She'd put one of herself in there, also, unable to bear the thought of her baby forgetting her altogether.

Peter stepped closer and held out his arms. For an instant, the image of that other time flashed through Jann's head. When she had flung herself into his arms and been wrapped in love and safety.

She wasn't safe now. This time his embrace was intended for Alex, not for her. When she let her baby go, it would be forever.

A moan involuntarily surged from her soul and lay trembling in her throat. At the sound, Alex buried his face against her shoulder. Then, with a movement so sharp it stunned her, he propelled himself forward into Peter's waiting arms, grabbing her crystal heart as he went, and ripping it from her neck.

He held his prize aloft, as an athlete would a trophy, and gurgled with glee. With a swift glance in her direction, Peter extricated the heart from Alex's fist and offered it back to Jann.

"Keep it for him," she choked out, blinking her eyes fiercely, not able, now, to hold back her tears. "My mother gave it to me. I want to give it to him. When Alex is old enough to understand, tell him that I love him."

"He knows that already," Peter said softly. Then he stared into Jann's eyes so long, she felt they could stay that way forever. "Come with us," he whispered.

She turned away, hot tears blinding her vision. "I can't," she said hoarsely. "There's nothing for me there."

Taking hold of her shoulder, Peter spun her around. "You're wrong," he said, seeming to want to say more. "Alex needs you," he said, instead.

Alex was only half of what she needed. With a hungry look at them both and mustering every ounce of courage she possessed, Jann plunged down the companionway and slammed the hatch shut.

It seemed a long time she stood in the cabin below, with her breath held so tightly she felt her lungs might burst. Until at last she heard Peter's footsteps fade away down the dock.

*   *   *

The days slipped painfully by. One week. Then two. Still no word. Not even a phone call to tell her they'd arrived in Boston safely. Nor a letter to say Alex was happy and adjusting.

Nothing.

But of course there would be nothing. It was over.

"You can't hide away forever," Ruby chided her briskly, sweeping onto Jann's boat like a miniature tornado. "It's not healthy." She lifted her too-wide sunglasses and peered down her nose at Jann. "You're skin and bones," she observed critically. "If you're not careful, you'll blow away."

Jann gazed bleakly up at her from the batch of photos she had just developed. The top one was of Peter grinning from behind the wheel of her boat. The one beneath was of him also, holding Alex on the day of the picnic. The leaden feeling in Jann's stomach intensified.

"Why don't you go to him, child?" Ruby suggested, her brown forehead creased with worry.

"You know why I can't." She bit her lip to keep from crying.

Ruby snorted. "Peter cares about you. More importantly, you care. You care about Alex and you care about Peter. That's reason enough."

"Peter doesn't love me," Jann said again, as she had said many times to her friend over the past two weeks.

Ruby snorted again, and her eyes seemed to magnify, to grow larger and larger until there was no escaping their pool of pity. The cabin walls, too, seemed to be moving in on Jann, suffocating her with their closeness, accusing her of cowardice. Her boat had always been a haven, but without Alex and Peter, it had become a prison.

She wanted to be with them, behind the stone walls of

Willow House if that was what it took, but she didn't have that choice. She had learned something over the past two weeks that she hadn't realized before, that it wasn't walls that made a prison, nor the lack of them that made for happiness. To be happy, she needed people in her life to love.

She needed Peter and Alex. Only they weren't available. Not to her.

"I'm going away for a couple of weeks," she said, her words stunning her, the result, she was sure, of too many sleepless nights. But the relief coursing through her convinced her the idea was a good one.

"To Boston?" Ruby asked hopefully.

"No." Slowly a plan took shape in Jann's mind. "Back to Maui." She'd been happy there—the last place she had been happy. Perhaps in work, her loneliness would disappear. "There are some photos—"

Ruby groaned.

Jann bit her lip.

"Pictures are no substitute for a man, you know."

Jann stared down at the photo lying in her hand. Ruby was right, but if she couldn't have this particular man, she didn't want any.

"I know," she said determinedly, laying the picture on top of the rest, "but I have to start somewhere."

Jann's bike missed the hood of a yellow station wagon by a hair's breadth as she cut into the lane in front of it. Her left turn signal a mere blur of hand and arm, she shot down a side street then into the park. Faster and faster she pedaled, glad the sidewalk was empty, glad also for the speed. Not ever wanting to stop. For when she did, she would have to face what she had done.

Her feet slowed. She would have to face it sometime. It might as well be now.

She stopped at Claire's bench, her fingers slick with sweat as she loosed her hold on the handlebars and dropped her bike to the grass. Her body was hot, too, though not only from exertion. The bench's smooth wood was soothing—Jann swallowed hard—but not soothing enough.

With a sigh, she pulled the envelope of tickets from her bag and spread them across her knee.

Boston, it said on the top one. Honolulu to Boston.

Maui, she had told the travel agent, yet here she was on a park bench holding tickets that would carry her over an ocean and half a continent.

All flights to Maui were booked until Monday, the agent had informed her. Something to do with high season, or was it overbooking?

But she had needed to go now, before the memories locked in her heart drove her demented. Like a rat in a maze, unable to escape, she had turned away. Then with no direction from her brain, she had turned back again.

"Boston," she had mumbled hoarsely, touching the bare spot on her neck, missing the counsel and strength of her mother's crystal. "Do you have any seats going there."

A clicking of the computer keys, a rapid printing of a page, and a ticket was in her hand.

With a soft moan, Jann stood, the adrenaline disappearing that had carried her this far. A chill prickled her arms and she shivered, a body-aching sort of shiver. Then, as suddenly and unexpectedly as the sun erases shadows, a warm glow erased the chill.

A friendly glow. A friend's glow. A Claire kind of glow.

She spun around, half expecting to see Claire sitting on the bench behind her.

But there was no one. An empty bench.

Yet the warmth was still there, surrounding her, comforting her. The same warmth Claire had always exuded, an approving kind of warmth, as though her friend was there, approving Jann's decision to allow Peter to take Alex, urging her also to follow them to Boston.

Peter didn't love her, Jann longed to scream, although she loved him with all her heart. How could she use this ticket if it was simply to cling to Alex? To be near Peter without his love would be unendurable.

Without knowing for sure how Peter felt: the glow seemed to answer, her life was already unendurable.

Grimacing toward the empty bench, Jann grabbed the handles of her abandoned bike and pulled it up and mounted it.

If she was going to go, and she suddenly knew that she was, she had to get home. There was so much to do: photos to develop, bilges to pump, instructions for John and Ruby as to which plants needed watering and to keep an eye on the battery levels . . .

She willed her whirling brain to a standstill. No sense fretting as though she'd be gone forever. It would take very little time to find out what she needed to know. Beyond that, she couldn't allow herself to think.


Even the cab drivers were different. No open-necked Hawaiian shirts or casual suggestions as to which beach had the best surfing. This Boston driver, despite the warm day, had his collar fully buttoned and wore a cotton jacket as well.

"A long way out of town," he had pronounced at the airport after glancing at the address Jann had scrawled on a piece of paper. "Might run to sixty dollars or more," he had added, casting a worried glance at her seen-better-days handbag.

Smiling with more firmness than she felt, Jann had handed him her knapsack. And now she was here, the cab sputtering through the twin gates to Willow House like the last racer to the finish line.

Peter's home was nothing like the orphanage. One more

thing she'd been wrong about. The stone wall around the property was crumbling in places, and ivy climbed over the top, just as Alex would climb when he was older.

And there were bushes flowering everywhere. Not the flamboyant, fragrant, Hawaiian flowers she loved so much, but others just as special. Azaleas and roses, clusters of impatiens, and forget-me-nots tucked in amongst the pansies lining the drive.

Gradually slowing as they neared the house, the cab shuddered to a halt in front of the steps. Jann climbed out, suddenly fearful to let the driver go.

"Wait for me," she said, stuffing her bag back into the cab's trunk, then resolutely climbing the stone steps to the front door.

One stab of the doorbell brought no answer, but that was hardly surprising with a house this size. Wishing for the hundredth time that she'd sent a telegram to say she was coming, Jann pressed the bell again.

This time, the door opened.

"Yes?" said the woman who answered, smoothing a voluminous blue smock over her wide hips while a cloud of graying curls fluttered back from her face in the breeze.

"Is Peter Strickland at home?" Jann asked.

"Yes," the woman replied, opening the door a little wider. The cluster of silver bracelets encircling her wrist tinkled against each other. "He's in the back garden. Whom shall I say is calling."

"A . . . a friend," Jann said, choking on the word. "I took care of his nephew in Hawaii." More than cared for him. Loved him.

"Jann Fletcher," the woman exclaimed, a smile sweeping the polite caution off her face. "I should have known from your picture." She held out her hand. "I'm Callie Reynolds, Alex's nanny."

Jann shaped her lips into a smile, her image of Alex's nanny as a cold, ordered woman dissolving. She'd been right to trust Peter. The sparkle in Callie's eyes and the smudge of flour on her cheek told Jann Alex's nanny was nothing like the dictatorial organizer of the orphanage in which she'd once lived.

"I'll take you right through," Callie said, laugh lines bracketing her eyes as her smile broadened. "Alex will be so happy to see you."

"Has he been homesick?" Jann asked anxiously.

"Not a bit of it," the woman denied with a tinkling laugh. "He has settled in beautifully."

"That's great," Jann said quietly, squelching a pang upon hearing he hadn't missed her.

"Follow me," Callie instructed, leading Jann down a beautifully proportioned hall, its warm wood paneling casting a glow on the glass fronts of the family portraits lining it.

Jann's face drained of heat. There on the wall, amongst past and present Stricklands, was the picture she had given Alex, the one of Claire holding her baby, her face filled with love.

The picture had been enlarged so that it was the same size as the others, and it looked so right sitting there, as though it belonged.

As she herself didn't belong.

"Beautiful, isn't it?" Callie said, following the direction of Jann's stare. Her expression softened. "I was only twenty when I first came to Willow House to look after Miss Claire. Seems a long time ago now."

Not so long, Jann thought. And Peter had been right. Callie had loved Claire. As she would, no doubt, love Alex.

"That picture of you," Callie said, smiling at Jann, "is next to Alexander's bed. It's the first thing he sees when he wakes up in the morning."

Joy erupted in Jann's heart. Maybe Alex wouldn't forget her. From somewhere in the house came the strident ringing of a phone.

"I'd better get that," Callie said, moving forward a few feet and opening a door on the right. "Mr. Strickland is expecting a call from overseas. Just keep going," she encouraged, "down the hall, through the sun room, and out the glass doors. You'll find them."

Finding her way was the easy part. Forcing her feet to actually move was much more difficult. With each step, Jann's worries multiplied as to what she would say when she finally faced Peter.

Stepping through the glass doors to the stone patio, Jann found an enormous rhododendron bush blocking her view of much of the garden. But in the far left corner, at the very edge of the lawn, was a willow tree, and beneath the tree was a bench.

With a man sitting on it, a folder of papers in one hand and a cup of something hot in the other. At his feet, sitting on the porpoise quilt she'd made, surrounded by his toys, sat Alex.

She took a blind step backward.

She'd been a fool to come, a fool to think either Peter or Alex was missing her. Loving her.

They had everything they needed. They had each other.

She fought back the images reeling through her mind, of the touches she and Peter had shared, the warm looks, the passion. False emotion, false dreams. The only real thing between them had been the heat, and that, she'd been told, could come and go as quickly as a flame to a match.

She should be grateful for the heat and leave it at that. Peter may not have given her his love, but the heat had been something she hadn't managed before. Perhaps next time . . .

Her throat closed over.

There'd be no next time. If she couldn't have Peter, she didn't want anyone else.

Turning, she stumbled back through the sliding windows. She had to escape, had to get away from this place.

"There you are, Miss Fletcher," Callie Reynolds said, entering the sun room and blocking Jann's way. "Couldn't you find them?" she asked, peering over Jann's shoulder. "Peter," she called, taking hold of Jann's elbow with one hand and raising the other hand and waving. "You have a visitor."

Peter read again the last words of the paragraph he was on, not wanting an interruption now. There had been too many friends visiting in the two weeks he'd been home, all of them armed with questions, with which they had curiously probed into the life Alex had led before he arrived at Willow House.

He couldn't sit and talk politely to anyone of Jann, the woman who'd cared for Alex and stolen his own heart. Jann's image already overran his mind at each waking moment, and at night in his bed, she ruled his dreams. To speak of her and Alex, and the life they had shared, only served to remind him of all he couldn't have.

With a sigh, he looked up.

"Jann," he said softly, his breath fleeing his lungs, the shock of seeing her standing there belting him in the gut.

She took a step forward, her dress floating around her legs. Like a mirage, he thought dazedly, shaking his head to clear it. His legs, when he stood, felt weak and uncontrolled, and he cursed that she'd come when he wasn't prepared.

With a great effort of will, he forced his body forward, gaining strength as he crossed the lawn to withstand her invasion of his heart.

"Hello, Peter," she said, when he got near enough to hear, her voice engulfing him in memories of soft nights and island music.

She looked at him uncertainly, seemed to withdraw into herself.

"You've got a phone call," Callie said from where she stood next to Jann. "The one you've been waiting for."

"Jann," he repeated gruffly, ignoring Callie's words.

"I've come to see Alex," Jann explained, her gaze shifting past him, searching the area behind him to where Alex still sat.

He should have guessed it wasn't to see him that she had come. This woman wanted nothing to do with the love he had offered, had turned him down in Hawaii. Nothing had changed.

"The telephone," Callie insisted.

Taking the call would get him away from Jann.

"I have to go," he said coolly. If only he wasn't plagued with the desire to hold her, if only he didn't care.

"I'll just be a minute," he added, thanking God for the excuse to get the space he needed to withstand Jann's spell.

He touched her arm, intending only to direct her across the lawn to Alex, but the shock when they touched was as overwhelming as it had been before. A desire engulfed him to tell her that he loved her, to take her into his arms and never let her go.

She jerked away before he could act, and he felt the loss of the contact with a pain that staggered.

His eyes were just as Jann remembered, as changeable as the ocean, and just as powerful.

"I've come to see Alex," she repeated, forcing her gaze from his. Only half the reason, not the whole. But she couldn't tell him now that she'd come to see him, for the caution in his eyes had just told her he didn't care.

Pain, sharp and piercing, shafted through her chest. If it was a miracle she had hoped for, those hopes were now dead.

Peter didn't love her.

Had never loved her. If she hadn't believed it before, she believed it now.

And it hurt. Much more than she had imagined.

"I don't have much time," she said, speaking the words swiftly, stiffening her body in an effort not to feel. "I'll just say hello to Alex and then I'll go."

"It's long distance, Peter," Callie interrupted, "from Paris."

"I have to answer that," he said. "But wait for me, Jann. We have to talk."

"There's nothing more to say."

"Promise me you'll wait."

Another promise for this family, and just as difficult as the one to Claire.

"All right," she agreed numbly. "I'll wait."

With that, he turned away.

Jann blinked as he departed, as though she'd been caught in a trance and had just now been snapped free. She turned toward Alex, needing with every fiber of her being to hold her baby in her arms once more.

She'd concentrate only on him, try to eliminate the other Strickland from her heart and mind.

With swift steps, she moved toward her baby. She would always think of Alex as her baby, no matter how far away he was or who he was with.

She said his name as she approached, was warmed through her pain when he looked up at her and smiled. Then Alex reached for her and her heart melted completely.

She picked him up slowly, his baby weight feeling wonderful in her arms once more. She longed to hold him forever, but knew that if she stayed more than a few minutes, it would be impossible to ever leave him again.

Why had Peter been so insistent that she remain here and talk? Did he want to impress upon her how well he and Alex were doing? Or did he want to discuss their relationship, make sure she understood that when they'd made love back in Hawaii, it had meant nothing to him.

Jann's body turned cold, except for the places where her skin touched Alex's. Her baby warmed her now as he had done after Claire's death. Losing Peter was like a death.

"You're looking very serious."

Peter had come from nowhere again, ambushing her heart just when she was trying to expunge him.

"Alex has missed you," he said, his voice low and strained.

"That's not what Callie said," Jann answered, not looking at him yet, not daring.

"She wouldn't want you to worry."

"No," Jann agreed. "She's very thoughtful."

"Why are you here, Jann?"

"I . . . I just decided to come," she said, determined not to let him know of the love that had spurred her action, love that would die now and whither like flowers in winter. "I thought I'd do some traveling." Her words were a lie, but all she really wanted now was to get as far away as possible, to make a break from this man who had destroyed her life.

"Traveling wouldn't have been easy with Alex in tow."

"No," she agreed slowly, but with Alex in her life, there'd have been no need of trips.

Coming to Boston had been a mistake. The only thing to do now was to return to Hawaii, to her friends and her boat, and the life she'd once known, to try with all her might to forget Peter and Alex.

"I'll just say goodbye to Alex," she said, sucking in a breath, determined Peter not see what she didn't want him to know, that without him and Alex she could barely go on.

"You just got here," Peter said.

His words seemed little more than the polite utterances of a stranger, not the friend she'd come to think him, and definitely not the lover.

"Everything happened so quickly in Hawaii," she explained. "I didn't get a chance to say good-bye to Alex properly." She was babbling, but couldn't seem to stop. "I wanted to see for myself that he was doing all right."

"I see."

One glance at his face told her he saw nothing, or whatever he saw, he wasn't sharing it with her.

"Alex's nanny seems nice," she went on rapidly, filling the growing silence with sound.

"Yes," Peter agreed. "Alex adores her. But . . ." His expression warmed for an instant and he nodded towards the child held in Jann's arms. ". . . I haven't seen him this happy since Hawaii."

Jann gently stroked Alex's hair back from his face and planted a kiss in the middle of his forehead. "It must be strange for him. A new bed, new people . . ." Her voice caught. She forced the words. "But he'll adjust. He's young. As long as he's fed, bathed, and held, he'll be fine."

"That's not what you said before."

"Isn't it?" She asked the question fiercely, tried to keep from her eyes the secret she carried, that she loved this man who had taken away her son.

"I've got to go," she said again, but desperately this time, the whole situation becoming more than she could bear.

"We haven't talked."

"We've nothing more to say." Unless they discussed the magic they'd felt that day in Hana, or the pools and the light and the love they had shared. Or did he simply want to say he was sorry they'd made love? If he did that, she couldn't bear it, for she wasn't sorry at all.

She thrust her baby back into Peter's arms, feeling the knowledge bite deep into her soul, that there would be no end of this for her, that she would love this man forever no matter what he felt for her. And nothing she could do or say would ever change that reality.

With one last longing look at Alex, she pulled her finger

free from his fist.

"No," Peter growled, catching her by the arm.

She stood motionless, trembling, engulfed in a fatigue of spirit that kept her feet rooted. Perhaps Peter was right. Perhaps she had to stop and listen. Maybe when she heard him say he didn't love her, had never loved her, the hard truth might release her heart. And after that was done, she'd be able to go home, back to her pictures and her boat and her life before Peter and Alex, back to a time when she didn't know all that love promised.

# Chapter Sixteen

Peter released her arm and gently placed Alex back onto his blanket. "You're going traveling?" he asked then, as though needing to lead gently into whatever he had to say.

"Yes," Jann lied, wishing he'd simply say it, so she could pick up the pieces of her broken heart and go home.

"But you'll be back?" he asked.

"I don't think so," she replied, pain battering her spirit like the winds of a hurricane. If she could capture that pain, she could turn it into strength. It was strength that she needed if she was ever to go on, if she was going to be able to let them go on too.

She realized suddenly that Peter held himself stiffly, as he had when she first met him.

"Take care of Alex," she begged, reaching out to touch Peter, unable to stop herself from the gesture although she knew it was useless.

"I will," he replied hoarsely.

She too had made that promise and it was one she'd been forced to break. She tried to speak, but her words strangled in her throat. Before she could force them out, his gaze gripped hers, and he cupped her chin and kissed her.

For one sweet single moment, she returned his kiss, finding neither the strength nor desire to push him away. Into that one delicious kiss she put her hopes, dreams, and promises; then, fighting a current of longing, she pulled loose from his arms.

"Be happy," she cried, then with a swift final glance at the two she loved, she turned and ran towards the house. She paused only once when Alex began to cry.

"Jann," Peter called after her.

She thought at first he would follow, then knew that he wouldn't when Alex's tears turned to sobs.

"Jann," he called again, more urgently this time, but in a voice muffled by the action of picking Alex up.

Hot tears blinded her eyes as she swept swiftly into the sunroom, then down the long corridor towards the front door.

Callie Reynolds emerged in front of her from a room off the hall, but Jann brushed past, ignoring the nanny's astonished look and out-flung arm. Even Claire's picture had no power to stop her, emitted no secret glow to force her back.

She'd been wrong ever imagining a life with Peter might be possible. She could only pray now that she'd be able to forget.

A swift opening of the front door, and an even swifter descent of the stairs brought her to the taxi. One look at her face must have told the driver her desperation, for he turned the key in the ignition, pressed his foot to the gas, and they roared through the twin pillars as though escaping the gates of hell.


Claire's bench was the same. And the view hadn't changed either. Even the sun was as fiery as before. But the magic was gone. As Peter and Alex were gone.

Jann dashed the beginnings of tears from her eyes. She couldn't cry any more. She'd been crying forever. Great bucket loads of tears that seemed to spring from her body as though from a secret reservoir.

No more. She was home now. Had to put her love behind her.

She had flown to San Francisco after Boston, thinking a few days there would give her time to think. But San Francisco with its misty bridges and clanging trolley rides was a city made for romance, not sadness. All she could think about was Peter, then Alex, then Peter again. Best to simply go home.

She shifted her bag to her other shoulder, glad she'd instructed the cab to drop her at the park. She wasn't ready to face Ruby and the Capt'n yet, didn't want to answer their eager questions and see the pitying looks in their eyes. She'd walk home slowly, decide what to say.

But once started along the sea wall, her feet moved of their own volition. She walked faster and faster until she was almost running, a kind of panic gnawing her chest that she recognized as fear.

Terror, that no matter how fast she moved, or how far away she lived, it would never be fast or far enough. That she could never outrun her memories of all she'd shared with Peter and Alex.

She glanced across the water toward the marina, thinking that if she could only see her boat, could get to *HEART'S DESIRE* swiftly, she might somehow be safe.

But she couldn't see a thing. Except for the light.

So much light.

Where was it coming from?

She stopped running, her legs trembling.

It was as if the sun—the warm and healing sun—had plunged from the sky and landed in the center of the marina. Prisms of radiance shone and sparkled, piercing the air with reflections off windows and metal, then scattering across the harbor in a multitude of rainbows.

Like magic.

Only she had thought the magic gone.

The light entranced and beguiled, reaching out and touching her, playing across her face and casting warmth into her soul.

It drew her towards home in the same way Peter had drawn her despite her fears. The closer she got, the brighter it became, as though all the light in the universe was concentrated on this special spot.

Walking through the marina gate, Jann started down the wharf. The light was coming from her dock.

Impossible!

From her boat.

Unbelievable!

Her feet froze. It was her boat. A fairyland of a boat. Crystal hearts hung from every stay, and they turned and swayed in the breeze, catching the sunlight, then shooting it back to the sky in rays of joy.

In front of the light was a man. A dark-haired, tall, lean mountain of a man. The light shot behind him and around him, even through him it seemed, lifting him towards her like a present from God.

Her heart ceased its beating.

Peter was the man.

With a fierce longing in her heart and a cry wrenched from her lips, she leaped across the inches of water and landed in his arms. When they closed around her, she knew she was home.

Finally . . . and completely . . . home.

She breathed in the scent of him, drowned in his touch, and with a tremulous sigh, gazed into his eyes. They were darker than midnight against the light, but clearer than morning.

"Thank God you're back," he said fervently. "I was beginning to think I might be wrong."

"About what?" she whispered.

"That you'd be coming home at all."

"I told you I wasn't."

"I almost believed you."

"And now?"

"You're here," he said simply, but there was satisfaction in his voice as though what he'd hoped for had turned out true. And something else was there also, a happiness that knew no bounds.

She couldn't examine such an emotion now, was afraid to look at it too closely lest it change shape into something else.

"How long have you been here?" she managed to ask,

terrified that if she spoke, the magic would somehow die.

"Two days," he replied, his eyes telling her it had seemed a hundred. "Since you left Willow House. I followed you to the airport, but the flight to Hawaii left before I could get there. I took the next one and have been waiting here ever since."

While she was in San Francisco, her heart as mournful as the screams of gulls.

"Happy birthday, my darling," he whispered, his arms tightening around her.

She couldn't think about him calling her darling, could scarcely believe he was here. She glanced instead at the crystal hearts, and to still her racing heart, began to count. One, two . . . twenty-six. She was twenty-six today. Had she forgotten or, like other years, had she simply not allowed herself to remember?

"How did you know?" she asked wonderingly.

"Capt'n and Ruby," he explained.

"I don't celebrate my birthday."

"You do now." He smiled gently.

How had she ever imagined his eyes were cold?

"Now, and for the rest of your life." He made the pronouncement as though it were a sure thing. Then he took her face in his hands. "With me," he added, "and with Alex . . ." Desire darkened his eyes. ". . . and with all the little Stricklands we can manage to produce." His expression softened. "If you'll have me, that is."

A cloud blew in front of the sun, blocking its brilliance, leaving only the light in Peter's eyes blazing down upon her.

"Do you love me?" Jann asked.

"Don't you know?"

"You said you never wanted to fall in love." She could still remember his eyes when he had informed her of that fact.

"I didn't. I changed my mind."

"What changed it?" she asked breathlessly.

"You did," he replied gruffly, "a thin slip of a woman with hair the color of a sunset."

She smiled. "You told me when we first met that I should cut my hair off."

"It attracted me," he explained, reaching out to touch a curl. "I didn't want to be attracted."

Which was how it had been with her, against her better judgment.

"Never cut it," he ordered, smoothing the curl with his fingers. "It's beautiful." His eyes darkened. "You're beautiful."

Her heart reeled.

"You never seemed to like me much," she said, wondering if this was a dream.

"I liked you," he said firmly, stroking first her shoulder, then down her arm. "But I was afraid."

She'd thought it was only her that knew the face of fear. Not this man before her with the strong arms and fearless heart.

His jaw tightened. "You were too much like my mother."

"No woman wants to be compared to her lover's mother."

"No." He smiled ruefully. "But you were both beautiful women. . ."

Beautiful. He had said it again. She hadn't simply imagined it the first time.

". . . who attracted people to them." He lifted one brow. "Even though you do your best to push them away again."

"I tried to push you away," she admitted.

"I was eager to be pushed."

"Because of your mother?"

He nodded.

"She left you and Claire."

"Yes," he said starkly.

She caught her breath. "Did you think I would leave too?"

"I was sure of it." His eyes darkened. "You lived on a

sailboat, dressed like a hippie, took photographs."

"The evidence is damning."

"Don't laugh," he said sternly. "My mother liked to think that she was an artist too."

"Was she?"

"No. She painted a little, but was really no good at it. Not like you with your photos. She mostly used it as an excuse to live a freewheeling lifestyle, to attend parties—"

"I don't like parties," Jann said emphatically.

"I should have guessed," he replied, laughing, then his eyes again turned serious. "But when I first met you, you seemed to be living the epitome of a gypsy life, no home, no car, no secure means of support. I figured that any minute you'd up anchor and sail away."

"Leave like your mother left?"

"Yes," he said again, "and I didn't want to be like my father, trying to hold on to something impossible to resurrect."

"What do you mean?"

"My father knew how my mother's absences affected Claire."

And Peter, too, Jann knew, sympathy wrenching her heart.

"So when she wanted to take off to attend an art show in Paris, he decided to go with her. He even chartered a private jet, no doubt thinking he could win her back, that if he shared her interests, she might share his."

"Is that when their plane crashed?" Jann asked softly, appalled by the pain Peter must have endured.

"Yes," he said, his skin paling beneath his tan. "For a long time I blamed my mother, both for her death and my father's." He gazed down at Jann, and his expression softened. "Then I met you."

Meeting him, loving him, had also healed her in ways she was just discovering, making her want to laugh and cry and exult in the joy of living.

"The only thing that mattered after I learned Claire was dead was the knowledge she had a son. I was determined to give him the life Claire had missed out on."

"One you missed out on too."

He shrugged. "I wanted Alex to have security, a place where he'd be safe."

"He already had that. With me."

"I didn't believe that at first." Peter gazed down at her, and smiled ruefully. "You looked like an exotic bird about to take off to God knows where, dragging my sister's child with you, or worse yet, leaving him behind. I couldn't allow that to happen."

"And now?" She caught her breath.

"Alex is not the only person I love."

Her heart exulted at his words. She held them within, letting them heat her from the inside out.

"Since my parents death," she said softly, "Alex has been the only thing in my life that has made any sense. Before he arrived all I did was work, convincing myself I was happy even though it wasn't true." The warmth from his love curled through her. "Then you came along."

"You treated me as though I were the enemy."

"You were the enemy," she said simply. "You wanted my baby, my life. But I soon realized you'd taken the one thing I least expected." She gazed into his eyes and found deep in their darkness an inextinguishable light. "My heart," she whispered, "and that terrified me."

"Why?" he asked, stroking her cheek with his thumb.

"If you loved me, you were doomed. Like my parents, and Claire. Or even more horrible, you might not love me back." She looked at him reprovingly. "You never said you did, even after we'd just made love."

"I couldn't," he said gruffly.

"Why not?"

"I didn't want to acknowledge, even to myself, that it was you as much as Alex that kept me hanging around Hawaii. I didn't want to admit I'd fallen in love with a New Age, heart-loving, crystal-collecting woman, who could end up doing what my mother did to my father. I couldn't risk it." He captured her mouth, and for a long moment there was no sound to be heard but the thudding of both their hearts.

"But you did risk it," she finally said.

"I couldn't stop myself. When we made love . . ." His voice trailed away, and in his eyes Jann could see the passion she'd seen flaming at the Seven Pools.

"You fell in love," she finished for him. As she had. Heart-stoppingly, irrevocably, forever and ever.

"Yes," he agreed simply, pulling her to him again. "I kept thinking it wasn't real, even praying that it wasn't. I thought if I got away from you, the feelings would disappear."

"Then Alex got sick."

"Yes."

"You were so strong." She swallowed hard. "You were the only thing that gave me hope Alex might be all right."

"It was your love that rallied him."

"Our love."

"Your crystal."

"So now you believe in crystals?" she teased, her voice shaky with emotion. Looking up into his eyes, she saw with joy his love and acceptance.

"Just trying to share your interests," he answered lightly back. Then the smile faded from his lips. "I believe in you," he said solemnly. "And if that includes crystals, or heart-shaped kitchen tables . . ."

She chuckled, the laughter warming her.

". . . then so be it." His expression darkened. "I wondered, when I heard of Claire's death, if things would have been different if I'd been there when she finished high school. If she could have come to live with me she might not have gone off to New York."

For a long moment she said nothing, wanting to weigh her words carefully, wanting to help this man who had helped her so much. "Someone once told me," she finally said, "that you can't predict what's going to happen." She fondled the hair at the base of his neck, reveling in its softness, and the warmth and suppleness of his skin. "You couldn't know." She shivered. "Everyone makes mistakes. I made a mistake when I didn't get the pipes on my boat fixed and look what happened to Alex."

"You didn't know," he said back to her, looking at her long and lovingly. "Maybe we both have to forgive ourselves."

His words filled her with a buoyancy that sprang from relief.

"I'm beginning to think you're perfect," Peter whispered, catching her to his chest in a way that rendered her breathless. "I love you, Jann," he said, staring into her eyes.

Her spirit soared at hearing the words she had so longed to hear, and she stared up at the twirling crystals. The shadows left in her heart cleared by the wellspring of light.

Peter loved her.

The twisting crystals told her so.

"Be my wife, Jann?" he added, with gut-wrenching honesty.

What if loving wasn't enough? What if loving couldn't stop her fears?

"You can't promise you'll be safe," she began, her voice near to breaking with emotion, hope, and fear intertwined, "or that Alex will either, or . . ." She couldn't say aloud what Peter had said before, that there would be more children than Alex to share their love. Their children.

His face was as strong as the frame of her boat. "Our love will keep us safe," he said firmly, staring down at her with eyes that never lied. "Together we'll make magic."

His words struck her heart. She hugged them there, savoring them, taking from them their strength.

"I was afraid once too," he went on, "afraid our love would turn out to be like that of my parents. I couldn't bear the thought, didn't dare take the risk. I prayed that once I returned to Boston, I wouldn't want you so much."

"I didn't think you did want me," Jann said, shivering at the memory. "When I turned up at your house, your face told me you wished me gone. You couldn't wait to get away to take your phone call."

"When I saw you," he said, "I realized for the first time that it was already too late. I knew then that I needed you more than the earth needs the sun."

He kissed her again, so thoroughly this time she thought his lips had become hers.

"Those feelings terrified me," he whispered, when at last he pulled away, "and when you told me you intended to take off on a world tour, I felt my worst fears had come true, that I'd lost you." For an instant bleakness once again engulfed his eyes.

"Not a world tour," she denied. "Not even a trip at all. I made it up, didn't want to seem pitiful."

"I couldn't bear to lose you again." His arms tightened around her waist. "When I realized how I felt, I couldn't let you go."

Her heart soared at his words.

"Even if we argue sometimes," he continued with a smile, "even if you make my blood boil."

"Even if," she agreed.

His smile deepened, a smile so full of love it pierced Jann's doubts and dispersed her fears.

"There was something I didn't take into account before I left Honolulu," he said, becoming grave. "When you love someone, you don't have a choice anymore. I could no more stop loving you than stop the world from spinning."

"When you asked me in Honolulu to come with you and Alex, I thought you wanted me simply for Alex's sake."

He leaned closer, his lips brushing hers. "I love you," he said, "in a way quite separate from all I feel for Alex. And strong," he went on, "oh, so strong." With that he captured her lips and sealed his words with a kiss.

"I love you, too," she whispered.

"Then you have to take a chance." He stared steadily into her eyes. "Risk everything, Jann, to gain everything."

"I love you," she said again, the words humming down her throat and vibrating in her heart.

Then all sound seemed to die.

But the light still shone down on them more brilliantly than before, filtering the air like a sprinkling of fairy dust.

It was a long moment before Jann could say anything more. It was enough just to hold and touch and join her heart with his.

"Be my wife?" he asked again.

His question resounded from her soul to her heart, then echoed back her love.

"Yes," she said firmly, glad of the light, the honest, piercing light, and the crystals that spun it for her heart to see. Catching hold of Peter's hand, she turned and faced the light, finally knowing her heart's future with glorious certainty.

– THE END –